THE
RUNAWAY
CLOWN

Adventures of the Northwoods

THE RUNAWAY CLOWN

Lois Walfrid Johnson

BETHANY HOUSE PUBLISHERS

MINNEAPOLIS, MINNESOTA 55438

Except for Big Gust, village marshall in Grantsburg during the early 1900s, and the visit made by the Ringling Brothers Circus in 1893, the characters in this book are fictitious. Any resemblance to persons living or dead is coincidental.

Cover illustration by Andrea Jorgenson.

Published by Bethany House Publishers
A Ministry of Bethany Fellowship, Inc.
6820 Auto Club Road, Minneapolis, Minnesota 55438

Printed in the United States of America

ISBN 1–55661–240–0

To Elaine

cherished friend,
and with special love to Daniel

LOIS WALFRID JOHNSON is the bestselling author of more than twenty books. These include *You're Worth More Than You Think!* and other Gold Medallion winners in the LET'S-TALK-ABOUT-IT STORIES FOR KIDS series about making choices. Novels in the ADVENTURES OF THE NORTHWOODS series have received awards from Excellence in Media, the Wisconsin State Historical Society, and the Council for Wisconsin Writers.

Lois has a great interest in historical mystery novels, as you may be able to tell! She and her husband, Roy, are the parents of a blended family and live in rural Wisconsin.

Contents

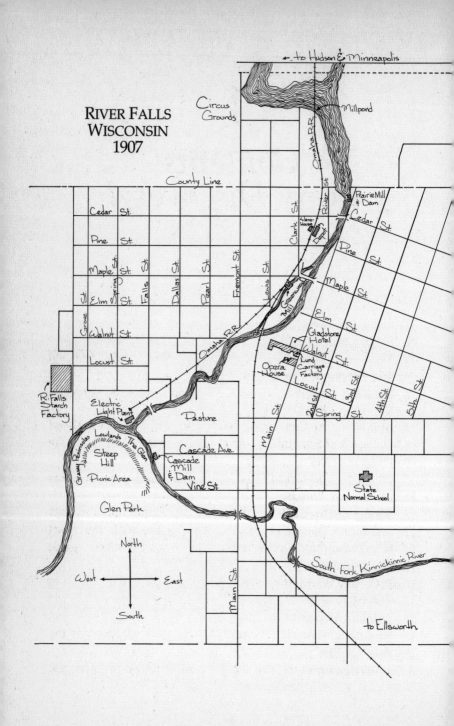

RIVER FALLS
WISCONSIN
1907

← to Hudson & Minneapolis

Circus
Grounds

Millpond

Omaha R.R.

County Line

Cedar   St.

Pine   St.

Maple St.   St.

Elm St.   St.

Walnut   St.

Locust   St.

Clark   St.

River St.

Ware-
house   Depot

Prairie Mill
& Dam

Cedar   St.

Pine   St.

Maple   St.

Elm   St.

Gladstone
Hotel

Walnut   St.

Lund
Carriage
Factory

Locust   St.

Spring   St.

Falls   St.

Dallas   St.

Pearl   St.

Fremont St.

Lewis St.

Greenwood

Mill

Grove   St.

Spring   St.

Omaha R.R.

Opera
House

Main   St.

2nd St.

3rd St.

4th St.

5th St.

R. Falls
Starch
Factory

Electric
Light Plant

Pasture

Grassy Peninsulas
Lowlands
The Glen
Steep
Hill
Picnic Area

Glen Park

Cascade Ave.

Cascade
Mill
& Dam

Vine St.

Main St.

State
Normal School

North

West ←→ East

South

South Fork Kinnickinnic River

Main St.

to Ellsworth

1

Scary Discovery!

*D*id you see *that*?" Katherine O'Connell grabbed her stepbrother's arm.

Anders shook off Kate's hand. "Don't hit my arm when I'm driving! You jerked the reins."

Even while Anders spoke, his horse Wildfire leaped ahead to what seemed a command. As the harness stretched tight, the farm wagon lurched.

Kate rocked backward. Next to her, Erik Lundgren braced his feet against the boards.

The mare moved into a gallop, and the wagon bounced over the dirt street. Kate clung to the edge of the seat, her heart pounding. At the railroad tracks, the wagon lurched again, swinging sideways.

Anders tightened the reins. "Whoa, girl! Whoa!"

Wildfire tossed her head.

"Whoa!" Anders called.

Panic clutched Kate's stomach as she glanced down at the wheels. *What if I fall off?*

Anders leaned back, pulling the reins with all his strength. "It's all right, girl! Slow down!"

Wildfire's ears turned to the sound of Anders' voice. This time the mare listened. As she passed between tall buildings, she finally slowed down.

"Dumb sister!" Anders exclaimed. "You could have started a runaway right on the main street of Frederic."

Deep inside, Kate still felt scared. Though she wouldn't admit it to Anders, she couldn't blame him for being upset. Along the street, people filled the wooden sidewalks. On that June day in 1907, it seemed that every farmer in northwest Wisconsin had come to town.

The minute Anders stopped Wildfire at a hitching rail, Kate jumped to the ground. Usually the Nordstrom family went to Grantsburg to shop. This morning Mama had sent them the opposite direction, to the village of Frederic.

As Erik snapped a lead rope onto Wildfire's halter, Anders' dog, Lutfisk, caught up to them. With his tongue hanging out, he panted in great gasps.

Trying to act as if nothing had happened, Kate flipped her long black braid over her shoulder. "Did you see the men putting up that poster?"

Without waiting for the boys, she hurried back in the direction from which they came. Lutfisk bounded along beside her.

At the cross street a man stood on a ladder that leaned against the end of the building. Using a brush, he smoothed a large sheet of paper onto the wall.

Another man stood on the ground, looking up. Kate walked around behind him, and Lutfisk followed. Planting his paws in the dirt, the dog pointed his nose toward the man and barked.

"Lutfisk!" Kate exclaimed. "Stop it!"

But Lutfisk growled low in his throat. The hair on his back stood on end.

"Call off your dog!" the man shouted at Kate. As though afraid of Lutfisk, he edged away.

The man on the ladder started down. "Aw, Leo, that dog won't hurt you."

"You wanna bet? You're a fine one to talk, Charlie. Way up on the ladder where he can't bite you!"

As though Lutfisk understood, he moved closer to Leo and bared his teeth. Suddenly the man kicked him.

Yipping in pain, Lutfisk tumbled over, rolling in the dirt.

"You— You—" Kate was so angry she could barely speak. "How can you *kick* an innocent dog?"

"He started it!" Leo answered as Lutfisk picked himself up.

"*You* started it!" Kate shouted. A hot wave of anger washed over her. "Lutfisk doesn't act that way with another person on earth!"

"Hah!" Leo snorted. "He probably attacks everyone he sees!"

Kate clenched her fists. "Lutfisk does *not* growl unless there's a reason!"

"Stop it, Leo!" Charlie stepped off the ladder onto the ground. "The girl's right. That dog wouldn't have hurt you."

Kate felt glad for Charlie's help, but Lutfisk pointed toward Leo. Once again the dog growled low in his throat.

"Be quiet," Kate commanded.

This time Lutfisk obeyed, but he edged close to Kate as though to protect her.

Kate knelt down and hugged him. Gently she felt his back and sides, checking for injuries. When her hand touched a tender spot, the dog whimpered.

"There's already a lump!" Kate exclaimed.

"That was a terrible thing to do," Charlie told Leo. "You tell her you're sorry."

"Sorry!" Leo scoffed at the idea. "Hah!"

"You're not going to keep your job very long," Charlie warned.

He turned to Kate. "I'm sorry, miss," he apologized. "The boss won't like this at all. He just hired Leo yesterday."

Kneeling down, Charlie reached out his hand toward the dog, as though wanting to make friends. "Lute fisk?" he asked. "That's a strange name."

Lutfisk edged forward, sniffed Charlie's hand.

"My brother called him that," Kate explained. "It's after the dried fish that Swedes eat at Christmas."

Leo picked up a bucket and stalked away from them. Still

keeping one eye on the dog, he slopped paste on the lower part of the building.

When Charlie stood up, he took a folded section of poster. He pressed one end against the wall, then unfolded the large sheet across the building.

"That sure looks easy," Anders said as he and Erik caught up to Kate.

"Easy!" Kate exclaimed. "That's because Charlie knows what he's doing." Quickly she told her brother what had happened.

When Anders felt Lutfisk's back, his face flushed with anger. "Say, mister," he said to Leo. "Don't you ever dare touch my dog again!"

As though agreeing with Anders, Lutfisk barked.

Leo swung around. "I still say you have a mean dog!"

Anders started forward, but Kate caught his arm.

"That's enough!" Charlie told Leo. "One more word and you're out of a job!"

As Leo returned to his work, Kate stared at him. His light brown hair was slicked back, away from his face, as though with grease. Just above his collar, the ends of the long strands came to a square point.

Like the tail feathers of a bird, Kate thought. The idea struck her funny, and she felt better.

Charlie worked air bubbles to the edge of the paper. Under his skillful hands the wall became a growing display of bright colors.

"That's what I thought!" Kate told Anders and Erik. "It's a circus!"

From the center of the poster a lion roared. Around the king of the jungle were other animals—elephants, bears, leopards, and monkeys.

"I've never seen a real lion or tiger." Anders studied the colorful picture.

"RARE WILD ANIMALS," he read aloud. "THREE BIG RINGS. TWO GIGANTIC SHOWS DAILY. FREE STREET PARADE."

On either side of the picture, Charlie pasted up large sections giving the name of the circus and the date.

"River Falls!" Kate groaned as she saw the town where the circus would visit. "That's at least sixty or seventy miles away! Do you usually advertise this far from where you'll be?"

"Nope!" Charlie glanced across the tracks. A passenger car with the words ADVANCE CAR waited near the station. "We went to sleep on a sidetrack. During the night someone hooked our car to the wrong engine. When we woke up, we were in Frederic, instead of River Falls."

As Charlie finished smoothing out the poster, Leo reached into a pocket and pulled out a handful of peanuts. Still watching Lutfisk, he cracked open a shell and popped the nuts into his mouth.

"Since we're here, we'll advertise!" Charlie said as Leo tossed the broken shell over his shoulder. "Under our Big Top we have the most daring acts ever performed!"

Charlie pushed back the hat covering his bald head and grinned at Kate. "Now, you just think, little lady, how much you'd like to come to our circus."

"And you want everyone to take a look at your posters," Erik said.

"Sure thing! We've got elephants so big you can't see around them. When we were a wagon show, we took one of them across the river on a ferry. The ferry *sank*!"

Kate laughed. She wasn't sure whether she believed Charlie or not. But his good humor was catching.

"What about horses?" Anders asked. "You have lots of 'em?"

"More than I can count," Charlie replied. "Baggage horses that do the work. White ring horses for tricks. And black ones, shiny as that mare you took down the street. You know how to handle a horse, young man. You'd be good in a circus."

Anders grinned, and Kate knew he was pleased.

"Why, we have a clown ten feet tall," Charlie went on.

"He walks on stilts?" Anders asked.

As Charlie nodded, Erik stepped forward. "Do you want us to help you? We could put a poster out in the country."

"How far out?" Charlie asked.

"Nine or ten miles." Erik glanced toward Kate and Anders. "Road cuts through their farm. Lots of people use it as a short-cut."

"Got a place to put it?"

"Right on their barn. Everyone going past would see it."

"Lots of people?"

"Yup," Erik promised him. "Bet all that work would be worth some free passes to the circus."

Charlie grinned, as though he wasn't surprised at the request. "Maybe it would at that." He reached into a pocket and came up with three tickets.

Leo gave Erik some large folded sheets, smaller ones with dates, and a bucket of paste. Then, as though glad to see the last of them, Leo picked up his brushes. Without a backward glance, he set off toward the railroad car. The minute he left, Lutfisk flopped down on his belly.

As Kate and the boys headed toward their farm wagon, Charlie called his farewell. "May all your days be circus days!"

On her way to the store, Kate set the folded sheets of paper in the back of the farm wagon. When the wind caught the edges, Erik weighed them down with the bucket of paste.

It didn't take long for Kate to find the things on Mama's list. As Kate set her packages in the wagon, she noticed a small piece of newspaper caught on the bottom of the paste bucket.

Carefully she separated the paper from the bucket. Someone had marked the corners of an article with a pencil.

TROUBLE FOLLOWS THE GREAT ROBERTO

In spite of efforts to keep back the bad news, the word is out. A trail of bad luck still follows the Great Roberto.

One year ago today, the trapeze artist plunged to earth in an accident that has not yet been solved. Though the famous aerialist escaped with his life, he was seriously injured. At the time, he told police that someone had tampered with his equipment. If this is true, the villain has never been found.

Because of his injuries, the Great Roberto can no longer work as an aerialist. Although he changed circuses, he once again is having unexplained accidents.

Fans of the Great Roberto can see him as a clown when the circus visits River Falls on July 13.

The Great Roberto, Kate thought as she finished reading the article. *Why does that name sound familiar?*

"What have you got, Kate?" Erik asked when he and Anders returned from the feed store.

"Something strange," Kate told him. "For some reason this bit of news was important to the person who saved it."

When Erik finished reading the article, he looked as troubled as Kate felt. "I don't believe in luck!" he said. "Especially bad luck!"

"Neither do I," Kate answered. "Someone is trying to hurt that man. I'd like to find out who!"

2

Sarah's Surprise

When Kate and Erik showed Anders the article, he agreed. "I wonder what's going on? It sounds like someone wants to get even with Roberto."

"More than get even. Really hurt him." In spite of the warm day, Kate shivered.

"Someone has to be really awful to fool around with trapeze equipment," Erik said.

Anders lifted Lutfisk into the back of the wagon. As he petted his dog, Kate saw her brother's eyes. She felt sure that Anders would rather have been kicked himself.

As he climbed up to the wagon seat, Kate again looked at the article. "*Unexplained accidents,*" she read. "Why are those words underlined?"

Anders shrugged. "Maybe whoever had the article wants those accidents to happen." He clucked to the mare, and she backed away from the hitching rail.

"But *why?*" Kate asked. Her stomach tightened as she thought about an innocent man getting hurt. "And why was that piece of newspaper stuck to the bottom of the paste bucket? Where did it come from?"

"The ground, I betcha." Anders turned Wildfire down the street. "It probably fell out of someone's pocket."

"We were the only ones around that bucket of paste," Erik said. "Us and those two men."

"Leo and Charlie." Kate liked Charlie. She didn't want to believe he would do something wrong. But Leo?

"Someone who would kick a dog might do an awful lot of dumb things," Anders muttered. He directed Wildfire onto a winding road.

"Oh!" Suddenly it dawned on Kate. "I know where I've heard that name before. The Great Roberto is related to Sarah."

"Sarah?" Erik asked.

"Sarah Livingston. My best friend from Minneapolis. She wrote about his accident. It really upset her."

Kate stared down at the words of the article. "Whoever is bothering Roberto has been doing it for a year."

"Maybe not for the whole time," Erik told her. "Maybe Roberto starts thinking things are all right, and then there's another accident."

Anders glanced down at Kate. Fifteen months before, his father, Carl Nordstrom, had married Kate's mother. Kate and Mama had moved from Minneapolis to Windy Hill Farm.

"It's like waiting to see if someone's going to pounce on you," Anders said.

On the narrow seat, Kate tried to edge away from her stepbrother.

"Coming up from behind you—"

"Stop it, Anders!"

"Reaching out, grabbing you from the dark!"

Erik laughed, but Kate didn't think it was funny. "One of these days, someone will pounce on *you*," she said. "Both of you!"

"Not me! I'm too big!" Anders sounded well satisfied with himself.

Erik grinned and pushed his wavy brown hair out of his eyes. He and his family lived on a farm next to Kate and Anders. Like

Anders, Erik was over six feet tall and had strong shoulders from doing farm work.

Although all of them were thirteen years old, Kate was small for her age and much shorter than the boys. Now she straightened to her full height. "It would be awful to keep wondering if something bad is going to happen to you."

"It would. And it might." Anders was still teasing.

On the way home they talked about the free tickets. "What good does it do to have them if we can't go?" Anders asked.

Kate couldn't think of anything more fun than a circus. Yet there wasn't enough time to earn money for the train. Then, too, if they could go, where would they stay?

"I've got an idea," Anders said. "River Falls is in Wisconsin, but it's just east of Minneapolis and St. Paul. If we figure out a way to go, you could meet Sarah for the circus."

Kate laughed. "Anders Nordstrom! For once you've got a *great* idea!"

"What do you mean, *for once*?" Anders offered his lopsided smile. "I can't think of anyone with more good ideas than me."

"Sarah would love to go!" Kate felt sure of it.

"And Michael!" Anders switched into a high voice, imitating a girl. "Michael Reilly would love to see you again!"

"Who's Michael Reilly?" Erik asked.

"Kate's old boyfriend from Minneapolis," Anders told him. Kate felt the warm flush of embarrassment creep into her cheeks.

In Minneapolis everyone had known that Michael liked Kate. Often her classmates teased, chanting in a singsong voice, "Michael's sweet on Kate!"

More than once Kate had told them to stop. Yet deep inside, she always liked the idea that Michael found her attractive.

Erik glanced away, as though trying to pretend it didn't matter to him. But when he took his gaze off the nearby trees, he had a strange look in his eyes.

Anders seemed not to notice. "Yup, Michael Reilly. Taught Kate how to pole a boat across the river. Now isn't that the kind of information it's important for her to know?"

"Well, it is—it was!" Kate said hotly. But she remembered

the ice skating parties in winter. The time she and Michael and their friends took a streetcar to Minnehaha Falls. Together they had walked down to the Mississippi, watched the boats come up the river.

Thinking about Michael again made Kate feel lonesome. For a long time she had wanted to become a great organist. But lately she had added something else to her dreams—a special boyfriend.

And someday— Kate hardly admitted it to herself. *Someday, a really special husband!*

"I'll betcha something," Anders went on. "I'll betcha good old Mike is still sweet on Kate." He looked across his sister to Erik. "I betcha he'd jump at the chance to see her again."

"I suppose," Erik growled.

For a moment Anders stared at his friend. As if suddenly realizing something, he started to laugh.

Kate jabbed him with her elbow. Anders choked on his laughter.

"Maybe good old Mike has another girlfriend by now." Erik sounded hopeful.

"Maybe," Anders answered. "But I doubt it."

He put both reins in one hand. With a great flourish, he pulled a big red handkerchief from his pocket and mopped his brow.

"True love—you know, it never dies!"

Kate laughed, trying to pretend she didn't care. Yet she wondered how Michael felt about her by now. Ever since leaving Minneapolis, she had wanted to see him again.

When they reached the trail that led into Windy Hill Farm, Anders stopped at the mail box. Erik climbed down and pulled out a letter. It was addressed to Kate.

"It's from Sarah!" Kate cried. "Maybe she already knows about the circus!"

Kate ripped open the envelope. Pulling out the letter, she read aloud.

Dear Kate,

This summer I've been staying in River Falls, helping my Granny because she hasn't been well. She's much better now.

This morning she told me that a few weeks ago a circus man came to town. He reserved a big empty lot and bought tons of food for the animals.

Granny said that a relative on my mother's side of the family now works for this circus. Do you remember when I wrote about the Great Roberto? He used to be a trapeze artist—one of the best aerialists in the world. Then he had a mysterious accident. I was at the show when he fell, and it was terrible.

Because he's always traveling, I don't see Roberto often, but I really like him. He's working as a clown now, but Granny says he's still having accidents—strange ones that can't be explained. It's as though someone is trying to get even with him.

You and your brother Anders have solved so many mysteries. Do you think you could help Roberto?

Kate looked up. "I was right! It *is* the same Roberto!" She continued reading.

The circus is Saturday, July 13, in River Falls. Granny says that if you can come, your whole family is welcome to stay here at her house.

Sarah's next words seemed to stand out from the paper. Kate stopped reading aloud.

If you can come, I'll invite Michael Reilly too. By the way, we call him M.R. now. It fits him better.

> *Your very best friend,*
> *Sarah*

P.S. M.R. still likes you.

Kate stared at the postscript. It was just what she hoped! Aloud she said, "I can't believe it! Sarah wants us to come!"

Anders grinned and shifted the reins into one hand. "All riiiiight!" Before Kate realized what he was doing, he grabbed the letter.

Frantically Kate clutched her brother's sleeve, trying to take the letter back. But Anders held it out over the edge of the wagon.

"Listen to this, Erik," he said. "Michael Reilly is M.R. now." Again Kate reached for the letter, almost falling off the seat. But her brother kept it at arm's length.

"Here's another bit of news!" he said. "M.R. *still* likes my little sister Kate!"

"Anders, you make me *so* mad!"

When Anders finally returned the letter, Kate's face felt hot with embarrassment. She glanced sideways, trying to see what Erik thought. He was looking at the trees again.

"How about that!" Anders said. "You want to solve another mystery, Kate?"

She did. *If someone's bothering a relative of Sarah's, I want to help,* she thought. But Kate was too angry at Anders to agree with him about anything.

Even more, Kate wanted to see her friends again. *I wonder if Michael is just as nice.*

M.R., Kate corrected herself. From now on, she'd practice saying *M.R.* so that she'd remember to use it.

As the winding trail took them through the woods, Kate glanced back over her shoulder. Lutfisk lay in the wagon bed with his nose between his paws. His sad eyes looked up at her.

"I sure don't like that Leo," Kate said.

"I can't stand him either," Anders agreed. He, too, looked back. "Takes a real mean guy to kick a dog."

"I wonder if we'll ever see him again," Erik said.

"I hope not." For the second time that afternoon, Kate shivered.

3

The Great Stiltwalker

As they drove out of the woods, Kate felt a welcome breeze. The trail passed close to the Windy Hill barn. Beyond that, the ground fell steeply away to Rice Lake.

When Anders opened the end gate of the wagon, Lutfisk jumped down. The moment the dog touched the ground, he took off for the pasture. Anders looked relieved.

As he and Kate and Erik finished putting up the poster, Grandpa hobbled out of the farmhouse. Only a few weeks before, he and Grandma had come from Sweden.

While on board ship, Grandpa had fallen, hurting his leg. Yet in the short time he'd been at Windy Hill Farm, he was walking better. Sometimes he even forgot to use his cane.

Grandpa studied the picture. "A circus?" he asked. In Swedish the word was the same, and Kate understood.

"Have you ever been to a circus?" Grandpa wanted to know.

Kate shook her head. After her Daddy O'Connell died, a circus had come to Minneapolis. Mama took Kate to see the free street parade, but they didn't have enough money for the show in the Big Top.

For a while longer, Grandpa stood in front of the poster,

looking thoughtful. Without another word he walked back to the farmhouse.

During supper the family talked about all that had happened that day. With everyone sitting around the kitchen table, Kate and Anders told about the circus.

When they finished, Papa said, "I'm sorry. We just don't have the money for train tickets."

But Grandpa turned to Kate's mother. "Since you were married, have you ever been away from the farm? For more than a day, I mean?"

As Mama shook her head, Anders translated Grandpa's words for Kate. She was the only one in the family who didn't understand Swedish.

"I have not given you a wedding present," Grandpa said to Mama. "I want to give one to your whole family."

"A wedding present?" Mama looked surprised. It had been more than a year since she and Carl Nordstrom were married.

"Remember the gold pieces the man gave me in Sweden?" Grandpa asked. "I still have money from that."

Grandpa looked at Grandma as if they had already agreed on what they wanted to do. "Emma and I will stay here and work," Grandpa said. "We'll take care of the farm while you're gone."

Kate's stepbrother Lars leaped up with excitement. Five-year-old Tina clapped her hands.

Mama's smile was soft. "We thank you," she said. "We thank you very much."

"We really can go?" Kate cried. It was a very unusual treat for a farm family to take such a trip.

"All of us!" Lars shouted.

"I will also pay for Erik to go," Grandpa said.

"Oh, good!" Kate blurted out. It was always more fun if Erik went along.

Anders turned to Grandpa. "I bet Kate would rather have Erik stay home."

Grandpa's slow smile spread across his face. "We'll let Erik go anyway."

When Anders translated what Grandpa had said, Kate felt a flush creep into her cheeks. She didn't have any secrets—not even from Grandpa!

———

After supper Kate found Anders and Erik outside the barn with some lumber and an old harness. When Kate noticed a tool for cutting leather, she asked what they were doing.

"Making stilts." Anders sawed a two-by-four into two lengths.

"Stilts! Whatever for?"

"So I can walk on stilts at the circus."

"You're tall enough as you are!" Kate scoffed. She was still angry about the way Anders took Sarah's letter.

"Yah, sure. This morning I measured. I'm six-one, almost six-two. With stilts and a high hat, I could be ten feet tall!"

"Even if you knew how to walk, they'd never let you be a clown!" Kate said.

"I want to try. If we're going to figure out a way to help Roberto, we've got to see what's going on."

Listening to Anders, Kate felt ashamed. With all her heart she wanted to help Roberto. Yet her brother's teasing had gotten in the way.

"The circus will be in town only one day," Erik said. "That's not much time to solve the mystery."

"One day!" That bothered Kate.

Erik pushed his hair out of his eyes. "What's more, we don't even know how a circus is *supposed* to run."

"Let's all try to watch everything that happens," Kate suggested. "Maybe we can figure out what's going wrong."

Anders and Erik worked together, nailing a wedge on the side of a two-by-four. On top of the wedge they nailed a small platform for a foot. Then, using buckles and leather from the old harness, the boys fastened four straps to each wooden pole.

When the stilts were finished, Anders sat down on a stump

near the barnyard fence. He buckled one strap around his ankle, another over his toes. The remaining two straps circled the calf of his leg.

As Anders stood up, he wobbled back and forth, then grabbed the top board of the high fence. From his great height he grinned down at Kate. Using the fence for support, he worked his way toward the barn.

On this side of the log building, the ground was firm and smooth. Moving his hands along the wall for balance, Anders walked the length of the barn. When he reached the far end, he started back to Kate and Erik.

"I did it!" Anders exclaimed when he reached them. A grin lit his face from ear to ear. "Now wasn't that a great idea?"

———————

As soon as breakfast was over the next morning, Papa Nordstrom took the big Bible down from the shelf. In his reading to the family, he had reached the sixth chapter of Daniel.

Kate knew the story well, but never tired of hearing it. While a young captive, Daniel was chosen to work in the king's palace. When King Darius wanted to appoint Daniel over the entire government, other leaders tried to get rid of him. They asked King Darius to pass a law. Any person who prayed to a god or man other than the king would be thrown into a den of lions.

Papa stopped reading and looked up. "Daniel kept praying three times a day, just as he did before. He even left his windows open so that anyone who wanted could hear."

"Wasn't he scared?" Lars asked.

"I think he must have been," Papa answered.

"But why didn't Daniel just close his windows?" Kate wanted to know. Just the thought of being thrown to lions frightened her.

Anders laughed. "Curious Kate! There she goes again!"

"But Daniel could have kept quiet about what he believed," Kate said.

"That's what a lot of people would do." Papa told her. "A

person with courage lives what he believes, even when it's hard for him."

A person with courage, Kate thought. *Would I ever have courage like Daniel?*

She doubted it. She knew how awful it felt to have someone like Anders tease her.

Papa read on. Though Daniel's king wanted to save him, Daniel was thrown to the lions. The next morning King Darius rushed to the den to find out what had happened. During the night, God had sent his angel to shut the mouths of the lions.

Long after Papa finished reading, Kate remembered his words: "So Daniel was taken up out of the den, and no manner of hurt was found upon him, because he believed in his God."

Just the same, Kate wasn't entirely convinced. *That was all right for Daniel, but what about me? What if someone I knew wanted to make things hard for me?*

Right then and there, Kate made a decision. *I know the smart thing to do. I just wouldn't say what I believe.*

Every day Anders practiced with his stilts. After walking along the barn for a while, he left the wall. Without any support, he walked to the nearby granary.

Watching him, Kate held her breath. If he fell, it would be a long way to the ground. He could even break an arm. Yet Anders made it safely to the small building and back.

"Just see how great I am!" Anders told her.

Walking on grass, he stalked toward the house. Without wobbling, he turned and started back on the trail that passed the barn. The bottom of his stilts left square pole marks in the dirt.

Kate had to admit her brother was getting good. Just the same, she wouldn't tell *him*. All week long, Anders had teased her. By now, Kate just wanted to get even.

As she watched, Anders picked up his speed. His long legs reached out until he was almost running. When he reached the barn, he said, "Wait and see! I'll be one of those clowns!"

"But why would a circus let you in?" Kate asked. "They have all their own people."

Anders glared at her. "Well, I don't have anything to lose by trying. I'll prove what a good stiltwalker I am!"

"Oh, you will?" Kate glanced at the fenced-in area back of the barn. An idea tugged at her mind.

"You've been walking in easy places," she told Anders. "What if it rains, and the circus grounds turn to mud?"

For the first time doubt crept into her brother's eyes. He shrugged it away. "I'll manage. You'll see."

"How do you know? Have you ever walked in mud?"

Anders looked around, as though trying to find an answer. His gaze lit on the soft ground back of the barn. Every day the cows drank water from a large steel tank. As they came and went, they left the ground water-soaked and mucky.

Ah-ha! Kate thought. *Maybe he'll land in the manure pile!*

Anders walked up to the fence. Bending over, he opened the gate and walked through. "Nothing to it!"

He stepped off along the fence, making good headway where the ground was firm. As he walked toward the watering tank, his left stilt sank into the mud.

For an instant Anders stood with one leg lower than the other. Then he managed to bring his right stilt forward. That, too, sank into the ground. The closer Anders got to the tank, the deeper the poles sank.

"You're going to fall!" Kate called as she hung over the fence.

Anders shook his head. "Not me!" Again he tried to raise his left stilt. This time it refused to come.

Anders rocked one way, then another.

Kate gasped. If Anders hit the side of the tank, he'd be really hurt. In that instant she felt sorry for what she'd done.

Her brother's arms waved wildly. Again he wobbled. Suddenly he tipped forward.

4

The Mysterious Stranger

*W*ith a mighty splash Anders fell into the center of the tank. Water sprayed out in every direction.

When Anders came up for air, his blond hair lay this way and that. Water streamed down his face. He grasped the sides of the tank, but his stilts made it impossible for him to stand up.

Kate giggled.

Anders glared at her. "It's not funny."

"Yes, it is." Kate giggled again. Finally she had gotten even! At the same time, she felt relieved that her brother wasn't hurt.

Anders leaned forward, struggling to take off his stilts. As he tried to unbuckle the wet leather straps, the water sloshed around him.

Kate couldn't resist rubbing it in. "Now you're *really* ready for the circus!"

Kate could hardly wait for that time to come. Seeing Sarah and M.R. again would make the circus even more fun. Because of train schedules, the family would be gone for four days. They planned to reach River Falls the morning before the circus.

The day they were to leave finally arrived. As Anders loaded the wagon for the drive into Frederic, Erik knocked on the kitchen door.

When Kate saw the look on his face, she stepped outside. "What's wrong?" she asked.

"I can't go."

"Can't go?" Kate wailed. "You'll miss the circus!"

Erik nodded. "My dad woke up with the flu this morning. He's very sick. My brother and I have to put up the hay, or we'll lose it."

Kate groaned. "Oh, Erik. I'm sorry!"

"I just can't be gone so long." Erik's face was filled with disappointment.

"It was your idea that got us tickets!"

Erik held his out. "Give my ticket to your parents. It'll be one less to buy."

Slowly Kate reached out her hand and took the ticket. "I wish you were going."

"So do I."

"We'll do something else," Kate said quickly. "When Anders and I get home, we'll think of something great to do." But even as she spoke, she wondered what could be as fun as a circus.

"Sure," Erik said again. He kicked at a stone, watched it spin across the yard.

Kate waited, wondering what he wanted to say. When he met her gaze, there was hurt in his eyes.

"About M.R.," he said quietly. "Do you still like him?"

This time it was Kate's turn to look at the ground. Like Anders, Erik sometimes teased until Kate could hardly stand the sight of him. Yet he'd also been a special friend. She didn't want to hurt him more.

"Kate?" Erik asked when she didn't answer.

"I don't know," she said finally. "I haven't seen him for over a year."

Looking up, Kate found Erik studying her face.

"Kate, when you come home—" He glanced beyond Kate toward where Anders was loading the wagon.

Erik lowered his voice. "When you come home, I'll be here. I'll still be your friend."

"Thank you," she said softly. This time she met Erik's eyes. More than once, he had helped her with something difficult or dangerous. Often she'd been glad for his . . . what was the word? *He's steady. I can depend on him.*

Now that idea made Kate uncomfortable. Again Kate looked away, fixing her gaze on a pine tree.

Dependable? That's what Erik was. Always there, the boy on the next farm. Yet what could be worse than being dependable, when M.R. always seemed so exciting?

When Kate glanced back, Erik looked even more unhappy. For an instant Kate wondered if he guessed her thoughts.

For the one hundredth time she asked herself, *What is M.R. like now?* She could hardly wait to find out.

———

"I can't get Roberto out of my mind," Kate told Anders as their train drew near River Falls.

At the back of the long passenger car, Papa had saved three seats. Kate and Anders sat in one of them. Across the aisle, Mama and Papa shared another. Mama held baby Bernie in her arms. Often she looked up at Papa and smiled as though this were the most special day in her life.

They're happy, Kate thought as she watched them. Even though she still missed Daddy O'Connell, Kate felt glad that Mama had married Papa Nordstrom.

Across from them sat Tina, Kate's five-year-old stepsister. Whenever Mama fed Bernie, Tina pretended she was feeding her dolly, Annabelle.

Next to Tina sat Kate's stepbrother Lars, who would soon be ten. A tuft of red hair stood up at the back of his head. The summer sun had multiplied his freckles.

Kate turned back to Anders. "Everyone else must have tried to figure out the unexplained accidents," she said. "How can we solve the mystery in just one day's time?"

Anders shrugged.

"And I keep wondering about that grouch, Leo. Lutfisk sure didn't like him."

"Dogs and babies," Anders answered. "They always know."

"Know what?" Kate asked.

"What Papa calls character—the character of a man."

"Do you think that's really true?" Kate asked.

Her brother grinned. "Should we try to find out?"

"If that newspaper article fell out of Leo's pocket . . ." Kate paused, thinking about it. "If Leo *does* have something to do with Roberto's unexplained accidents—"

"If, if, if!" Anders sounded impatient.

"Do you suppose we'll see Leo again?"

Anders shook his head. "I doubt it. Someone who works with advertising needs to stay ahead of the circus."

"I hope you're right. Or maybe the circus fired him. I can't believe they'd let him stay after what he did to Lutfisk."

Kate fell silent, thinking ahead to the next day and the circus coming to River Falls. Soon even her questions about Leo dropped away. Sarah had written back, promising to meet them at the train depot.

Kate could hardly wait to see her. Fifteen months before, when they said goodbye, they had promised each other they'd always be friends.

Maybe Sarah's changed, Kate thought now. She tried to push away her uneasiness, to tell herself they would just take up where they left off.

Soon the train slowed down to crawl across a trestle. Kate saw water on both sides of the bridge. Then a long whistle warned people at a crossing.

Within minutes brakes squealed. Cars clanked together as the train came to a stop.

———

From the doorway of the passenger car Kate looked around. At the edge of the group of people waiting to meet passengers, Sarah stood by herself.

"There she is!" Kate exclaimed.

Sarah's pink dress made her honey-blond hair seem even more lovely. She had pulled the long strands away from her face, then allowed them to fall in soft curls down her back.

Behind Kate, Anders let out a soft whistle. "You didn't tell me that she's beautiful!"

Up until now Kate hadn't realized it herself. Had Sarah changed that much in fifteen months? Or was it just that they hadn't seen each other?

Sarah had grown at least three or four inches taller than Kate. *She looks sure of herself,* Kate thought as she started down the steps. *She even wears her dress longer than I do.* According to the fashion of the day, the length of Sarah's skirt was a sure sign that she was growing up.

In that moment Kate felt very young. Never before had she felt embarrassed about the clothes Mama sewed for her. After all, her mother had been a dressmaker in Minneapolis. But now Kate wished she could somehow make her skirt longer.

Then Sarah waved.

Kate hurried toward her, threw her arms around her friend. "I could hardly wait to see you!"

Sarah hugged Kate, yet stepped back almost at once. "It's been *forever* since you left Minneapolis!"

"Sarah?" Kate asked, then felt afraid to go on. For the first time in her life Kate wondered if Sarah didn't want to be hugged.

Behind Kate, Anders cleared his throat, clearly wanting to be introduced.

Kate turned to him. "Sarah, this is my brother Anders."

Sarah's smile lit her soft brown eyes. It wasn't hard to see how Anders felt.

Watching her friend, Kate felt glad she had brought along her white dress. On Sunday she'd wear it to church, and maybe M.R. would think she was pretty too.

Sarah led Kate's family to a hack—an enclosed wagon with windows all around and two long seats facing each other. The horses took them between tree-lined streets to the west side of town.

There Sarah's grandmother lived in a big house with an open

porch across the front side. In the lot directly back of the house was a barn.

Granny wore her gray hair drawn back in a bun. Wire-rimmed glasses perched on the end of her nose. "Welcome!" she told all of them. "Welcome!"

She squinted through her glasses at Kate and Anders. "Sarah tells me you've come to solve Roberto's problems!"

Anders raised an eyebrow and winked at Kate. She felt sure she knew what he was thinking.

"We really want to help Roberto," Kate told Granny. "But we can't promise that we'll figure out what's wrong."

"Fiddlesticks!" Granny waved her hand at the idea. "If at first you don't succeed, try, try again." She seemed to have no doubt about whether they'd manage.

Granny led them up the steps to the second floor, talking all the while. She settled Lars and Anders in a bedroom they would share with M.R. when he came.

Kate carried Bernie to another bedroom. There Mama pulled out a dresser drawer, set it on the floor, and lined it with a soft blanket. The moment Kate laid the baby down, he drifted off, as though he were in his own little cradle.

Kate and Tina shared a third bedroom with Sarah. The large windows opened onto two sides of the house—one of them overlooking the street.

"M.R.'s coming tomorrow morning!" Sarah told Kate the minute they were alone. "You know, he was the most popular boy in our class this year."

Kate wasn't surprised. Every girl in school had wanted M.R. to notice them. *And he always paid attention to me!* Kate hugged the thought to herself.

In that moment it seemed like old times with Sarah telling Kate a special secret. For the one hundredth time she wondered, *What will it be like, seeing M.R. again?*

Often they'd gone swimming in one of the Minneapolis lakes. Michael would yank her braid just to get her attention. Even when she pretended she didn't notice, Kate knew everything he was doing.

Then Granny called, and the moment with Sarah ended.

———————

After supper Granny led the family to the big front porch. Kate sat on the top step, watching Sarah and Anders talking together on the steps below her. Since the moment they met, Anders had found plenty to say to Sarah. By now Kate felt left out.

"Let's go for a walk," Anders said when the shadows grew long across the street.

Sarah jumped up as though glad to be doing something. "I'll show you River Falls."

Kate stayed on the step. More than once since reaching town she had tried to talk with Sarah. Always there seemed something between them, almost like an invisible wall.

She's supposed to be my friend, Kate thought now. Yet she wasn't sure if Sarah wanted her along.

Then Sarah turned. "Aren't you coming, Kate?"

Lars went with them, too, and Kate wound up walking with him. Much as she liked her younger brother, Kate again felt left out by Sarah and Anders.

Sarah led them past blocks of houses and down a steep hill to the Cedar Street bridge. Along the way, she explained the things they saw. Anders drank in every word.

"This is the Kinnickinnic River," Sarah told them as they stood on the bridge. Swiftly moving water flowed beneath them—water darkened by the growing dusk.

"Kin-nick-kin-nick?" Kate could hardly pronounce the name.

"Granny says it's an Indian name."

Upstream Kate saw the Prairie Mill and a large dam. Beyond the dam, the river widened into a pond. Kate recognized it as the one they had crossed on the train coming into River Falls.

On Main Street she was surprised to see electric street lights—lights powered, Sarah said, by an electric plant farther along the river. Yet even now, after the sun was down, the lights were dark.

Sarah explained why. "On moonlit nights they don't turn them on."

As they strolled along Main Street, Kate noticed a stranger ahead of them. His footsteps sounded hollow on the wooden sidewalk. Though well dressed in a suit and hat, there was something strange about the way he acted.

Farther along the street, the man glanced back. In the darkness he was too far away for Kate to see his face. Just the same, she couldn't stop watching him.

What is it? she wondered, bothered by what she didn't understand.

Hurrying on, the man stayed close to the tall business buildings, in the shadows where it was darker.

Kate caught up to Anders, pointed to the stranger.

"I know," her brother said quietly. "I've been watching him."

Ahead of them, light streamed from a lantern set in a window. As the man drew close, he pulled his hat lower, then swung out, farther from the building.

Where there's less light! Kate thought.

Even so, the lantern light showed Kate something she hadn't seen at first. The pockets of the man's suitcoat bulged out at both sides.

Again Kate felt curious. She had faced enough mysteries to know when someone made her suspicious. *Why is that stranger sneaking around in the shadows?*

5

Growing Danger!

When the man reached the Gladstone Hotel, he picked up his pace, moving even faster. Farther along the street, he suddenly disappeared between buildings.

"What's he trying to hide?" Kate asked.

Anders shrugged, but the look in his eyes showed Kate that he, too, felt curious.

All the way back to the west side of town, questions whirled around in Kate's mind. Could it be that the stranger had something to do with Roberto? It didn't seem possible, yet Kate felt sure that the man didn't want to be seen.

At Granny's house, Papa was sitting on the front porch. A kerosene lantern on a small table next to him shed light on his newspaper. Kate dropped down beside him.

"How are you doing?" Papa asked when everyone else went to make popcorn.

"Fine," Kate answered, though she felt just the opposite. She was still uncomfortable about the way Sarah acted.

Is it just that she likes Anders? Kate wondered. *Or is there something wrong with me?* Strangely, Kate felt pushed aside.

Papa put down his newspaper. "What's bothering you?" he asked.

His question reached Kate where she hurt. "It's Sarah," she said.

"Is she different from what you remember?"

Kate nodded. "We always told each other everything—even our best secrets. Now she seems far away."

"Sometimes that happens when people don't see each other for a while. You live in different worlds now."

"But what should I do?"

"Keep reaching out," Papa said. "Maybe Sarah's shy."

Kate laughed at the idea. "Shy? Not Sarah. She's always sure of herself."

"Maybe. But there might be a little place inside Sarah where she doesn't feel quite sure of things."

Kate sighed. She doubted it. Much as she wanted to believe Papa, her uncertainty about Sarah increased her worry about M.R. *What if he sees me and doesn't like me anymore?*

Kate flipped her long braid over her shoulder, then pulled it forward and twisted the end. Her worry spilled out.

"How does a boy know if he should marry a girl? And how does a girl know if she should say yes?"

Papa's eyes looked thoughtful. He picked up his coffee cup, sipped slowly. "Whether you're a boy or a girl, it comes down to the choices you make," he said finally. "When you meet someone, you choose whether you like that person. Whether you want that person to be a special friend."

More than once, Kate had felt that way about Erik. But now . . . even in her thoughts . . . Kate had left Erik home on the farm.

"If you meet someone special, the more you see him, the more you'll like him," Papa said.

Kate's thoughts leaped toward Minneapolis. When she lived there, she had liked M.R. so much that it was awful to move away.

Would he ever ask me to marry him? If she got the chance, Kate knew what she'd say.

"When you choose a special friend, it's important that you believe the same way about God," Papa went on.

Kate had seen Mama and Papa doing just that. Yet Kate felt uneasy. For the first time she wondered, *What does M.R. believe?* They had never bothered to talk about it.

"There are other things too," Kate said quickly.

Papa nodded. "A husband and wife should have things they like doing together."

Relief filled Kate. She and M.R. always had fun together.

"They need to be able to talk about things," Papa said. "Even things they don't agree on."

Kate felt even better. She and M.R. always agreed on everything. And they never had a bit of trouble talking. In school they passed notes back and forth.

"There's a way to avoid a lot of hurt." Papa set down his coffee cup. "It's better not to let yourself get serious about a boy unless you think the same things are important."

"Like God?"

"Especially what you believe about God."

Like a bothersome mosquito, Kate's uneasiness returned. *I've changed this year—changed in the way I believe. What if M.R. doesn't like that?*

Kate thought a moment, then decided. *I'm just not going to tell him.*

"Maybe we should start praying about who your husband might be," Papa said.

Kate tried to act as if his words weren't important. Yet her thoughts raced. *When I get married, it's going to be to someone as exciting as M.R. Maybe it'll even be him!*

Just then Kate heard Anders coming through the hall behind her. Still turned toward Papa, Kate raised her voice so her brother could hear.

"You better pray about who Anders marries," she said. "He's going to need an awful lot of help."

———

Early the next morning Kate heard a soft knock outside the bedroom she shared with Sarah. When she cracked open the door, Anders and Lars stood in the hallway.

"Hurry up!" her younger brother whispered. "The circus train will soon be here!"

"We're ready," Kate answered. "Let's go."

In the half-light just before dawn, she and Sarah hurried with the boys to the depot. A long train had just pulled in.

Directly behind the locomotive were several animal cars. Next came the long silver flatcars that carried circus wagons, then the passenger cars.

The locomotive backed the train onto a sidetrack, uncoupled the cars, then pulled away. At the end of the string of flatcars there was an open space for unloading.

As Kate watched, the circus men placed a wide ramp at the door of an animal car. One by one, dapple-gray horses came down the ramp.

"Percherons!" Anders exclaimed. He was always interested in whatever horses were around.

The large draft horses were already in harness. On the dirt road next to the tracks, men hitched them into teams.

"They're baggage stock!" said a barefoot boy who was part of the growing crowd of onlookers. Like Kate, he had the deep blue eyes of the Irish.

"Baggage stock?" Lars asked.

"They take circus baggage around." The boy's straight red hair was long on his forehead. "The wagons, tents, poles. Everything. Baggage horses do all kinds of work."

The boy's name was Darren. He seemed about Lars's age. "First time to see a circus?" he asked.

Lars nodded, his eyes wide as he tried to take in everything.

"Sure, and if I can't show you around," Darren said.

He led them to a grassy slope where they could watch the circus wagons being unloaded. At the end of the first long flatcar, men set down two narrow ramps called runs.

The men also placed flat pieces of steel between the cars, creating a "road." One at a time, the wagons rolled from one flatcar to the next, pulled by a rope from a team of horses walking on the ground.

A man steered each wagon by holding the pole at the front.

As a wagon rolled to the end of the flatcar and started down the runs, the poler scrambled ahead.

"What if a wagon rolls too fast?" Kate asked Darren. "The poler is right in front of it."

"See that man?" Darren pointed to a worker with a block of wood on the end of an iron handle. As a wagon rolled across the flatcars, the man on the ground walked alongside.

"If he needs to stop a wagon, he'll throw that block in front of the wheel."

As Kate watched, she noticed something else. A rope hooked onto a ring on the end of the wagon led to a steel post in the center of the flatcar. A man with strong-looking arms worked there, wrapping the rope around the post.

Darren called the man a snubber because he worked at a snubbing post. The rope he held kept a wagon from running away.

Kate gave the snubber a second look. Though all the other circus men were clean-shaven, he had a stubby beard. His battered hat was pushed back, and his dark brown hair almost reached his glasses.

During a pause between wagons, the snubber reached into his pocket. When he pulled out a red handkerchief, a peanut shell came with it.

As the shell dropped to the ground, something nudged at Kate's mind. She tried to remember how Leo looked.

About the same height, she thought. *Maybe the same weight.* But Leo did not have a beard, nor a battered hat and glasses.

Then, too, the color of the snubber's hair was wrong. It was also longer than hair could grow in two weeks.

With his handkerchief the snubber mopped his sweating forehead. As he pushed his glasses higher on his nose, his gaze settled on Kate, then shifted to Anders.

"I don't like the way he looks at me," Kate whispered when the man returned to his work.

Anders grinned. "He probably knows you're as curious as a cat."

Kate didn't think it was funny. "I just wonder what he's up to."

One bright red wagon after another left the runs. In the grow-ing daylight the crowd of onlookers was getting larger. People pushed into the unloading area.

"Stand back! Stand back!" a circus worker called to the on-lookers.

Kate turned to Darren. His Irish speech made Kate lonesome for her Daddy O'Connell. Though she had grown to love Papa Nordstrom, she still hurt inside whenever she thought of her father.

"You know a lot about the circus," Kate told Darren.

"Aye. That I do." It would have sounded like bragging, but Darren was serious. He seemed proud of all he had learned.

"How do you know so much?"

"Sure, and if I'm not here every year! Da always took me—"

"Your father?" Kate asked. She looked across Darren and saw that Sarah was listening too. "Where's your da now?"

Sudden tears appeared in Darren's eyes. "He died this spring."

For a moment Kate stared at Darren, unable to speak. As if pictures were flashing in front of her, she remembered the days after her Daddy O'Connell died. Once again she felt empty. She ached with knowing he would never again come home.

"I'm sorry," Kate said softly. "My daddy died too."

"He did?"

"It's pretty awful, isn't it?"

Darren nodded. His tears spilled over, ran down his cheeks. He tried to wipe them away.

"I wish Da was here now." Darren spoke quickly, as if trying to prove he was all right. "I wish he could tell me about the circus, the way he always did."

Kate swallowed around the lump in her throat. "Since he isn't, why don't you explain for *us*?"

Again Kate glanced toward Sarah, then back to Darren. "Tell the rest of us everything you know. Everything your da told *you*."

Darren's bare feet shifted on the grass. He seemed to want to be strong, even about the way he stood.

In the open space at the end of the runs, the driver of a six-horse team waited. Wearing a bright blue knit top, he rode on one of the horses. As onlookers pushed forward, the rider waved them back with his hand.

This time the crowd obeyed. The man in the blue shirt brought his team closer to the runs.

In that moment, Sarah called to him. "Hi, Roberto!"

The man on horseback grinned and waved. "Hi, Sarah!" he shouted. "Come see me when I'm through working, all right?"

"So that's Roberto!" Kate exclaimed. The man sat on his horse as though he enjoyed driving a team. "I thought he was a clown!"

"He is," Sarah said. "Since his fall, I mean. If a circus is short of help, people do more than one job until everything gets done."

Kate poked Anders and pointed Roberto out. But Anders was already watching how Roberto handled his six horses.

When Kate looked back at the flatcars, a large wagon covered with canvas was rolling across. For an instant the snubber glanced toward Roberto, then gradually let out his rope. The man guiding the pole leaned over, steering the wagon.

As it started down the runs, the wagon lurched forward. The poler scrambled, staying ahead. In the next moment, he lost his hold and stumbled.

When he tried to jump out of the way, the corner of the wagon caught his leg. The man tumbled off the run and lay still.

6

More Questions

*O*h!" Sarah clapped her hands across her mouth. But she could not hide her fear.

Among the onlookers, a woman screamed.

As suddenly as the bandwagon slipped out of control, it shuddered to a stop. From the ground near the runs the poler moaned.

Kate caught her breath. She didn't want to look at the man's pain. Yet the next instant she started forward to see if she could help.

Anders stopped her. "They'll have someone who knows what he's doing."

Roberto jumped down from his team of horses. Kneeling beside the injured poler, he gently felt the man's leg.

"Is it broken?" someone asked.

"I don't think so," Roberto answered. "But get Doc!"

The other man headed off on a run.

"Roberto," Anders said quietly to Kate. "With another accident."

"Do you think that wagon was meant for him?" Kate whispered. "It was the poler who got hurt."

Anders looked grim. "If the wagon had gotten away, it would have rolled straight into Roberto's team. Anything could have happened."

Sarah looked scared. "Someone is still trying to get Roberto," she said.

Only then did Kate remember the worker controlling the rope. When she looked in that direction, he was gone.

"The man at the post," Kate said. "The snubber."

"I know," Anders said. "When did he leave?"

Kate shook her head. In the excitement she had also missed his slipping away.

The poler moaned again, then opened his eyes. Moving his head, he looked around, as though wondering where he was.

"Where does it hurt?" Roberto asked.

The man pointed to the leg Roberto had checked. He tried to move, but flinched against the pain.

"Take it easy, Slim," Roberto told him.

Sarah turned to the others. "Roberto helped me once when I fell down," she said. "I was just a little girl, but I've never forgotten.

When the injured man tried to push himself up, Roberto asked him to wait until they knew what was wrong.

"Slim is a clown." Darren was watching the man on the ground. "What a grand fellow he is! He walks on stilts."

"Is that right?" Anders asked.

"Last year he wore an Uncle Sam outfit. Walked the whole parade, picking up wee lads and lassies. He shook hands with some of the older lads. That's how I got to know him."

Soon a man carrying a black doctor's bag hurried up. "What happened?" he asked.

As the doctor examined Slim, Roberto explained. When the doctor pushed up Slim's pant legs, Kate saw a scraped and bruised leg.

"Could have been a lot worse," the doctor said. "I'm glad the wagon didn't roll over you."

Before long, two more men arrived. They carried a stretcher—a blanket stretched between two poles.

Again Slim tried to get to his feet. Instead, the men lifted him onto the stretcher. As the doctor led the others to a passenger car, a worker hitched the bandwagon to Roberto's team of horses.

"That accident shouldn't have happened," Darren said. He sounded like a wise old man. "That snubber let the rope out too fast."

"You're sure?" Anders asked.

"Aye, I'm sure. Good thing that man threw the block in front of the wheel. It could have been real bad."

Kate had been so busy watching the poler that she missed the rest. Yet she remembered one thing. "Just before the accident, the snubber glanced toward Roberto."

Sarah looked at Kate, her brown eyes troubled. "Do you think—"

"Maybe," Kate said. "But if the snubber *is* the problem, we have to find out if he caused other accidents too."

"And we have less than a day to do it," Anders reminded them. "I want to talk to Roberto right away."

When Roberto signaled his horses to move out, Anders started after him. Kate and Sarah and the boys followed.

At Cedar Street five- or six-inch ruts scarred the dirt road, still wet from rain two nights before. Roberto directed his horses up the long hill.

In a short distance the heavy wagon wheels were thick with layers of mud. The large Percherons strained against the harness.

Roberto pulled his horses to a halt. Soon a team of eight horses with a man riding on one of them came down the hill.

The new driver hitched his team ahead of Roberto's. Pulling together, the fourteen horses moved the heavy bandwagon up the hill.

As Kate and the rest followed the wagon, Sarah told them more about Roberto. "He was the most exciting trapeze artist I've ever seen. It was like he *flew*! He did all kinds of things I've never seen other aerialists do. But then he fell!" Sarah shuddered, as though she didn't want to even think about it.

When the long hill evened out, a man unhooked the extra

team from the bandwagon. Roberto turned his horses off Cedar Street onto a grassy lot.

There a pattern had already started to take shape. All the circus workers seemed to know where to go. Alongside what Darren said was the cookhouse tent, men unloaded tables from a wagon.

As Roberto pulled ahead, Anders followed. A sharp whistle stopped him. A man on horseback pointed, telling him to get out of the way.

Just behind Anders was another wagon, this one carrying long poles. Kate felt sure they had to be for the Big Top—the huge tent for the big show.

The driver turned his team toward the center of the lot. Halfway there, the wagon suddenly lurched to one side and stopped.

"Whoa!" the driver called. The two right wheels had found a soft spot, sinking hub-deep into mud.

Again the man on horseback whistled, held up his arm and signaled with his fingers. Two more teams of eight horses moved in to help. As the horses pulled forward, the wagon rolled up and out of the mud.

By now Roberto had slipped from sight. "Where do you think he is?" Anders asked.

Sarah shook her head. "Let's ask for the dressing tent."

They soon discovered that the tent where clowns and other performers changed into their costumes wasn't up yet. No one could tell them where Roberto was.

Anders looked worried. "If Roberto doesn't already know, he needs to be warned."

"But how?" Kate asked. "We can't warn him if we can't find him!"

"We'll keep searching," Anders said. "You were right, Sarah. It really looks like someone is trying to get even with Roberto."

Before long, the huge center poles of the Big Top were unloaded and set in place. Men and elephants worked together to pull great rolls of canvas near the poles. Other men with heavy sledgehammers pounded stakes into the ground.

Men laced the canvas sections of the tent together. Working

swiftly, they tied the canvas to rings at the center poles. Once again, the elephants went to work.

As the huge tent rose from the ground, Kate felt as if she couldn't believe her eyes. It seemed like a miracle the way the Big Top mushroomed from the earth.

At the edge of the circus lot, the river widened into the mill-pond Kate had seen on the way into town. A team of horses pulling a water wagon came from that direction. Partway across the lot, the wagon mired down in mud.

This time the man on horseback signaled for elephants. As they lumbered toward the water wagon, their trunks swung from side to side. Each time they moved, they left a large hoof print in the soft dirt.

When the elephants reached the wagon, their handlers set down big, round tubs, like the one Kate's family used for their Saturday night bath.

Darren ran forward. "I'll water 'em for you! My friend will help." He motioned for Lars to come. "It's good for a free pass to the Big Top."

Darren opened the faucet at the back of the wagon. He and Lars filled the tubs with water. The elephants drank with their trunks, sucking up water and emptying it into their mouths.

To Kate's surprise they didn't all look alike. Not only were the elephants different in size, but also in their shape and the appearance of their eyes.

Never before had Kate been close enough for a good view of an elephant's baggy skin and huge toenails. Their hair was as stiff as wire.

After drinking awhile, an elephant lifted its trunk and sprayed water all over Lars.

Lars shouted with laughter. On that warm July day, Kate knew it must feel good to be wet.

"That's Carrie!" Darren exclaimed. "I knew her from last year."

Suddenly the elephant reached out and wrapped her trunk around Darren's waist.

"Anders!" Kate cried. "Do something!"

Before anyone could move, the elephant tightened her grip. In the next instant, she swung Darren up, high in the air.

7

M.R.

*H*elp!" Kate called to the handler.

But Darren laughed. He patted the elephant as if she were an old friend.

"She remembers me!" Darren stretched out his arms, but couldn't reach around the big head. "What a wee lass you are!"

Carrie seemed to enjoy herself as much as Darren. After a few minutes she gently lowered the boy to the ground.

"Can Carrie really remember for a whole year?" Kate asked the handler. She had often heard that elephants were intelligent.

The handler grinned. "Well, you saw what she did. But she might remember her tricks better than a person. I know one thing for sure: An elephant won't forget someone who's been mean to her."

The elephants continued drinking until it seemed they couldn't possibly hold another drop.

As more and more wagons rolled onto the lot, Anders again asked for Roberto. Finally one man said, "You know, we're short-handed, and Roberto's good with a team. Maybe he went back to the train."

Anders pulled out the pocket watch Papa had loaned him.

He turned to Sarah. "What time is M.R. coming from Minneapolis?"

"9:45."

"We have to hurry."

With long strides Anders started across the lot. Kate needed to take three steps for every two of his.

Though it was still early in the day, Kate already felt warm and dirty. "Wait a minute," she said to Sarah and Anders.

Kate wished she had gone back to Granny's to clean up. She hurried over to the water wagon and opened the faucet. Letting the water run, she washed her hands.

"Hey! Don't waste it!" called one of the men as water poured on the ground.

Quickly Kate shut off the faucet and rubbed her hands over her face. That was better. Just being wet felt good. She'd look nice for M.R.

Kate ran to catch up with Anders and Sarah. As they reached the edge of the circus grounds, Kate heard a faraway whistle. The train would soon be here!

Already crowds of people lined Cedar Street, all of them dressed in their Sunday best for the circus. At the bottom of the hill Anders led the girls, cutting across a lot.

Again the train whistle shrieked, this time from close at hand. Moments after they reached the depot platform, the locomotive puffed into sight.

As the brakes squealed, Kate pushed back the hair that had fallen into her eyes. She smoothed her mauve dress and straightened to her full height. Holding her head high, she practiced smiling.

Hello, M.R., she said in her imagination. Her voice would sound just right—soft and ladylike and grown-up, yet somehow like a girl he would long to know better. *I just hope that he thinks I'm pretty!*

After a few other passengers stepped down, M.R. appeared in the doorway. His black hair waved back from his face. Like the boys and men around him, he wore a white shirt and a suitcoat.

Kate's heart leaped. M.R. looked even more handsome than she remembered!

As he walked toward them, Anders sniffed, then sniffed again. "What's that funny smell?"

"Be quiet, Anders!" Kate muttered. Why did her brother always have to embarrass her?

Anders sniffed a third time, so loudly that it sounded as if he had a cold.

"Shush!" Kate commanded.

"But that smell—it's like perfume." Anders spoke in a low, but carrying voice. Then light broke across his face. "It's his hair!"

Kate hurried forward, eager to be away from her brother. But when she reached M.R., she suddenly felt shy.

M.R. stopped directly in front of her. When his warm smile flashed across his face, Kate's fear fell away.

"I've really missed you," he said.

Kate's heart melted, as if in a puddle at her feet.

"I've missed you too," she answered softly, looking up into his eyes.

M.R. reached around, yanked her long braid, and Kate remembered. It had been their signal whenever M.R. wanted to tell her she was special.

Quick tears blurred Kate's eyes. She blinked them away.

Then Anders was there. Before Kate could introduce the two boys, her brother offered his hand. "Anders Nordstrom," he said, his voice full of confidence.

M.R. clasped his hand, grinned at the taller boy. "Kate's brother, I suppose?"

Though M.R. didn't say it, Kate felt sure he had heard the comment about his hair.

Anders glanced toward Kate, raised one eyebrow, then turned back to the other boy. "Mike Reilly, I suppose?"

"People call me M.R.," he answered. He, too, sounded confident, as though he was not the least bit afraid of anything Anders might try.

Kate wanted to giggle. When she first met Anders, he had made her feel like fighting about anything that came up. She wondered if M.R. felt the same way. Yet he seemed ready to ignore whatever Anders might try.

Like Sarah, M.R. also seemed older, and Kate didn't think it was just the clothes he wore.

"Hey, we better get our places for the parade," Anders said.

He started toward Cedar Street, where they were to meet Mama and Papa. Sarah seemed happy to go ahead with him, and M.R. fell into step beside Kate.

But M.R. walked slower, as it he wanted to talk. "You know, Kate, when you moved away, it was really hard."

As though it were yesterday, Kate remembered how she had missed him. "You were always such a good friend," she said. "Remember how we met in third grade?"

On the school playground a bully had started to tease her. Though he was a whole head taller, Kate was ready to fight back. Then Michael stepped between them.

"What are you doing, picking on a girl?" he had asked. The bully never bothered Kate again. From that time on, M.R. had been her friend.

Now he grinned. "What I remember is how you always managed to get into a fight. In sixth grade you even were sent to the principal's office!"

From deep inside, Kate's laughter bubbled up. "But you were there first! You were the start of it all!"

As they left the depot behind, M.R. stopped. It seemed as if he couldn't take his gaze off her face.

"Kate . . ." He paused. For the first time since she had known him, he seemed afraid to speak.

What does he want to tell me? On that warm beautiful day, Kate felt as if birds were singing from every tree. Whatever he wanted to say, it had to be really wonderful.

"Kate . . ." Finally M.R. plunged. "Whatever is wrong with your face?"

"My face?"

"You have a dirty ring all around the edge of it."

8

Desperate Chase

*L*ike a piece of glass, Kate's pride shattered in every direction. She remembered the man at the water wagon telling her to not waste water. *Did I wash my face too fast?*

Frantically Kate pulled out her handkerchief and rubbed around the edge, next to her hairline.

When Michael tried to help her, she shook off his hand. "I've never been so embarrassed in my whole life!"

M.R. laughed. "You're awfully pretty when you blush, Kate."

"Am I all right now?" she asked.

"More than all right." His eyes met hers.

Together they hurried to catch up with Anders and Sarah. When they reached Cedar Street, Lars and Darren waved to them. On the other side of the road, they had saved places. Mama, Papa, Tina, and the baby were already there.

Here, along the parade route, people stood ten and twelve deep with children in front where they could see. Men wore hats, white shirts, and suitcoats. Many of the boys also wore white shirts and suitcoats.

Seeing how well dressed they were, Kate wondered if Darren's mother had enough money to buy him shoes. Though many children went barefoot all summer, almost everyone had shoes on today.

Kate took a place with M.R. on one side and Darren on the other. Beyond Darren stood Lars, then Anders and Sarah with the rest of the family. When Kate introduced Lars, her younger brother looked M.R. over just as carefully as Anders had done.

A woman wearing a huge hat with clusters of silk flowers stood in front of Kate, blocking the view. When Kate looked at the hat and made a face, M.R. grinned back. Edging away, he gave Kate room to move over.

Where they stood, the ground was level. A short distance to their left, the land dropped away in the straight up and down banks of the Kinnickinnic River. People coming from Main Street still crossed on the narrow bridge.

Around Kate, some of the families had brought large baskets of food. One mother took out a pint jar of milk and poured her small son a drink.

Nearby, another child grew restless. "Is it coming soon?" she asked her mother every three minutes. "Is the parade coming?"

Before long, Kate heard the clear tones of a bugle. She peered up the long, steep hill on her right. As the sound moved closer, a rustle of excitement moved through the crowd.

Moments later, three buglers in red, white, and blue uniforms appeared over the crest of the hill. Red feather plumes decorated the bridles of their white horses.

Not wanting to miss a thing, Kate leaned forward into the street. Against a cloudless sky, the riders lifted their bugles in a fanfare that drew the crowd's attention.

As the buglers rode down the hill, three other men, also on white horses, followed with American flags. Next came five ladies wearing red and white flowing dresses, riding sidesaddle.

From beyond the hill, Kate heard a spirited march that set her toes tapping. Closer and closer the music came. Then a brass band appeared, riding inside the top of a white bandwagon decorated with gold leaf.

The driver sat on the high seat, the reins for eight horses between his fingers. Beside him, a helper held the brake wheel.

At the crest of the hill the wagon stopped, and a circus worker hurried into the street. He took something from the side of the wagon and laid it in front of the left rear wheel.

"What's he doing?" Kate asked Darren.

"Putting down a drag shoe—a piece of iron. It's like an extra brake. Slows down the wagon—makes the wheel skid instead of roll."

The wagon stopped again at the bottom of the hill. Another worker pulled what Darren called a let-go-quick release. The man hung the drag shoe onto the wagon and signaled the driver to go on.

As the huge wagon passed nearby, the music stopped, and Kate heard a deep knock from the wheels. Red, orange, and yellow webs of wood filled the spaces between the spokes, giving a sunburst of color. Then the music started again—a lively circus march.

Alongside the next wagon, a clown did cartwheels so close to the hooves of the horses that Kate gasped. "How can he do that?" she asked.

"They're Percherons," Anders reminded her. "Good, steady horses."

Kate studied their dappled-gray sides. Certainly there was plenty to get a skittery horse nervous. In the July heat, women fluttered white handkerchiefs, trying to stir the air. Not far away, a firecracker exploded. In spite of the constantly moving crowd, the draft horses stepped on.

Soon the wonderful sights started to blur together. Each time something came by, Darren told Kate and Lars all about it.

"How do you know?" M.R. finally asked the boy.

Kate waited, wondering if Darren would talk about his father again. Instead, a mask slipped down over his face.

"Oh, I just know." He looked away as though he didn't want to answer.

From that time on, M.R. answered Kate's questions. Before long, she glanced at Darren. In spite of the excitement all around him, he stood quietly. With hands in his pockets and shoulders hunched over, he stared at the parade.

M.R. hurt him, Kate thought. Just as quickly she pushed the idea aside.

M.R. wants to talk with just me. She felt better then, even pleased that M.R. wanted her to himself. Yet she ached for the younger boy, who was seeing the parade for the first time without his father.

As soon as she could, Kate leaned close to Darren. "Will you tell me about the next wagon?" she asked softly.

Darren's deep blue eyes brightened. He pulled his hands from his pockets and strained for a better look up the hill.

"That's the tiger cage coming," he said with great satisfaction. "See the number on the front?"

As Kate looked, she saw a large 37.

"Every wagon has a number," Darren explained. "And each wagon has a special job to do."

Soon another bandwagon appeared with clowns sitting high inside the top. As squeaks and squawks shattered the air, people laughed and cheered.

Far above the crowd, a trombone player stood and waved. When the wagon stopped for its drag shoe, the player threw up his hat, then caught it on the end of his trombone. As the wagon moved on, he tossed the hat again.

In that moment the wagon lurched. The hat fell onto the dirt street far below. The clown wiped his eyes, as though crying.

A small boy ran out to pick up the hat. But in the next instant, the wagon rumbled forward, faster than it should on the steep hill.

"Stay back!" the clown yelled to the boy.

"That's not part of the act!" Anders muttered.

As the wagon picked up speed, the clown fell backward inside the high top. The left rear wheel skidded on its drag shoe. Slowed down by the shoe, the wagon turned at a strange angle.

Frantically the helper turned the brake wheel. The driver pulled back on the reins. Band instruments disappeared. Clowns clung to the side of the wagon, staring down. On the steep hill, the wagon swayed.

"They're going to tip!" Darren cried.

Two clowns jumped from the back end of the wagon, rolling in the dirt as they landed. Moments later, three more jumped to the street.

Partway down the hill, a chain snapped, flying out at the rear wheel. The wagon jerked forward and straightened out. With nothing stopping it, the wagon rolled ahead, out of control.

"The river!" Kate exclaimed.

As the wagon picked up speed, it rocked from side to side. The horses struggled to stay ahead of it.

"Run!" a man shouted.

Papa snatched up Tina. Mama ran with the baby.

"Lars!" Kate called. "Darren!" Together they raced away from the oncoming wagon.

Suddenly Kate wondered about Sarah and M.R. Filled with panic, Kate looked back. As the bandwagon reached level ground, the terrified horses raced ahead in a gallop.

Just then Anders ran out into the street, directly in front of the runaways.

9

Hide-and-Seek Enemy?

$\mathcal{A}$ moment later, Anders changed direction. For an instant he ran alongside the nearest lead horse. His hand reached up, grabbed the bridle, held fast.

"Whoa, there!" he cried as the horse pulled him off his feet. "Whoa!" Anders shouted again as he touched ground. "Settle down."

The horse tossed its head, as though trying to shake Anders off. But Anders hung on. His feet again swung off the earth.

Just short of the bridge, the horse wavered, then slowed down. When he and the other lead horse stopped, so did the rest of the team.

Looking stunned by what had happened, the people turned toward Anders. A hush fell on the crowd.

The horse held by Anders shuddered. In the stillness a baby cried.

Then a man cheered. The crowd broke out in applause. But Anders still clung to the bridle as though his life depended on it.

"Whoa, there!" he commanded again. Once more, the frightened horse shuddered, then stood quiet.

The driver handed the reins to his helper and scrambled down from the high seat. As he hurried forward, Kate ran into the street.

"Are you all right?" she asked Anders. A line of blood ran down his cheek from a scratch on his forehead.

"Yup." Anders grinned, but kept his hands on the bridle. "Be careful, Kate," he warned. "Percherons are steady, but they've had a bad scare."

As she stepped back, Kate looked up at the nearest horse. Its eyes rolled as though still terrified.

Just then the driver caught up to Anders. His clown makeup hid his face, but his voice was filled with gratitude. "That was a mighty brave thing to do!"

He clapped Anders on the back, then took the bridle. As he led the team to the right side of the road, he asked, "What's your name?"

When Anders told him, the clown offered his hand. "Roberto here."

"Roberto?" Anders looked startled, and Kate moved closer to hear.

The man nodded. "I don't drive a wagon unless we're short-handed. You know my name?"

"We're here with Sarah," Anders explained. "I've been trying to find you since the accident at the runs. I don't think it was an accident."

"Shhhh!" Roberto warned. He looked around as though making sure that no one else could hear.

Anders lowered his voice, spoke quietly. "I think you'll find something wrong with the brake chain. And the chain for the drag shoe too."

Roberto's brown eyes widened. While another circus man held the horses, the clown circled the bandwagon.

Kate pulled out a clean handkerchief and handed it to her brother. As he pressed the cloth against his forehead, the bleeding stopped.

Staying clear of the wheels, Roberto looked under the bottom side of the wagon. Anders followed, kneeling down beside him.

When they finished their inspection, neither of them spoke.

"Come to the dressing tent after the parade," Roberto said. "I want to talk to you."

As the rest of the parade passed around, a circus man pulled out tools and crawled beneath the bandwagon. Working quickly, he connected the drag shoe safety chain, then the brake chain.

When the worker said the wagon was safe, Roberto climbed back up to the high seat. At the next opening he reentered the parade.

"How did you know there was something wrong with the wagon?" Kate asked Anders as they walked back to the other side of the street.

A grin lit her brother's face. "My dear sister, I've lived on a farm all my life."

"The wagons aren't the same."

"But I've learned whatever I could from Papa. About any wagon, I mean."

When they reached Papa, he clapped Anders on the shoulder. "Good job, son. I'm awfully glad you're all right. And I'm proud of you."

Just then a man on horseback started down the hill.

"Hold your horses!" he shouted. "Here come the elephants!"

Near the warehouse across the road, men hurried to their farm wagons. Other men clung to the bridles of their saddle horses.

Again the circus man shouted, "Hold on to your horses!" After the near disaster, no one needed the second warning.

The huge elephants walked single file down the street. A boy wearing a white helmet sat on the head of the lead elephant. The trunk of the next elephant clung to the tail of the first. The rest of the elephants shuffled past, trunk to tail.

As the last of the elephants passed them, Tina's eyes sparkled with amazement. "Look at their tracks! Their feet are *this* big!" She clasped her hands above her head, holding her arms in the biggest circle she could make.

After the elephants came the calliope* with a smokestack

---

*Pronounced *kall*-ee-ope by circus people.

belching black smoke. Through an opening in the side of the wagon, Kate saw a number of whistles. A man sat at a keyboard, a cloud of steam billowing around him.

The music sounded as loud as a factory whistle. As the notes of "Yankee Doodle" poured out on the street, Kate pushed aside her shaky feelings. For that moment she forgot about the runaway bandwagon.

What is it like, playing so the whole world can hear? she wondered as she watched the calliope player. She would do her best to find out.

Kate looked up at M.R. and grinned. Then she remembered he didn't know about her wish to be a great organist. The minute she got a chance she would tell him.

————

As the calliope passed by, Kate sighed, sorry that the parade was over. The crowd of onlookers poured into the street. More than once, someone talked to Anders, thanking him for what he had done.

"Let's follow the parade!" Darren said.

Already a crowd of children trailed after the belching calliope. Kate fell into line with the others. With the shrill whistles shrieking ahead of them, they walked across the Cedar Street bridge. On the other side they turned onto Main Street.

In the business section of town the calliope rattled the windows. After passing the Lund Carriage Factory and the Opera House, the parade turned left at Cascade Street. Like a Pied Piper the calliope drew children along, running to keep up.

A few blocks farther on, a large building appeared on their right. "That's the State Normal School," Darren told Kate.

"What's a Normal School?" Kate asked.

"They train teachers. The best thing they teach is the music. When the windows are open, I sit outside, listening."

Kate looked at the building with new interest. Built of red brick and trimmed with light-colored sandstone, it was three stories high, in addition to the basement.

Sarah dropped back from where she walked with Anders.

"That's where I'm going to go," she said. "I'll become a teacher."

As the parade turned left onto Fourth Street, Kate turned back to look at the Normal School again. *I could teach music!* She had thought so often about being an organist, it hadn't occurred to her that she could do more besides.

"Oh! Susannah" the calliope shrieked as it traveled north to Cedar Street. There the elephants and calliope turned back toward the circus grounds.

Kate and Sarah started up the big hill together. As Anders and M.R. walked ahead, Kate could hear what they said.

M.R. clapped Anders on the back. "Hey! You're a hero!"

Anders looked at him as though wondering if the other boy was pulling his leg.

"You sure took a chance on that horse!"

Anders shrugged. "Well, someone had to. Papa would have, but he had Tina and Mama."

"You could have been hurt—really hurt."

Listening to them, Kate felt glad that M.R. seemed to like her stepbrother.

————

When Kate and the others reached the circus grounds, they found a tent city had gone up since they left. A line of banners— large pieces of cloth that advertised what was in the sideshow— led people to the entrance of the sideshow.

"Step right up!" a talker called. "Step right up, ladies and gentlemen! The biggest, most stupendous, most colossal attractions you'll see in your entire life!"

Beyond the sideshow was the red wagon where tickets to the Big Top were sold. Already a long line of people waited to buy their way into the afternoon show.

Kate looked around for Darren and Lars. Somewhere along the way, they had lost them.

"They'll be fine," Anders said. "They're having a good time together."

He led the rest of them around the ticket wagon. Beyond lay the large tent where circusgoers viewed animals in their cage wagons.

Near a canvas door, a man stopped Anders. "We're not open yet."

"Roberto told me to find him after the show," Anders answered quickly.

"Ah! You're the one who stopped the runaway horses. We're grateful to you!"

Word of the near disaster had already spread, for when the guard called to someone else, the man said, "Right this way, sir."

As the man lifted the canvas door, Anders turned to Sarah and Kate. "You notice that," he said in a low voice. "I'm a sir now." Anders winked. "Pay attention."

The worker took them into the backyard, the area where circus people did everything that was needed to run the show. Usually the backyard was off limits to those who came to the circus.

The worker led Anders toward the dressing tent. The canvas door and part of one wall was open, as though to catch any breath of air. A curtain hung between the men's and women's side of the tent.

Roberto sat on a bench with a bucket in front of him, washing his hands. He had already changed out of his polka-dot clown costume and removed his makeup.

When he saw Anders, Roberto leaped to his feet. "Thank you, thank you, thank you!"

Quickly he wiped his hands on a towel and held them out to Sarah. "How's my favorite relative?"

"I'm glad you're feeling better," Sarah answered.

"Can't get a good man down." Roberto grinned, but the smile didn't reach his eyes. "How's Granny?"

"She wanted to be here," Sarah said. "She's been sick and isn't up to it yet."

Sarah drew Kate forward to introduce her. "Kate and Anders have solved a lot of mysteries. They want to help you."

"If we can," Kate added quickly. "If you want our help."

Roberto shook hands with them, as well as with M.R., then turned back to Anders. "Well, you've done us a big favor already!"

To Kate's surprise Roberto asked no questions about the accidents of the morning. Instead, he said, "The flag is up on the cookhouse. Let's go eat!"

Inside the big tent, red and white checked cloths covered the long tables. Roberto led them to an area where other performers were eating.

When the food arrived, Anders seemed to forget even Sarah. He ate two full plates of roast beef, potatoes and gravy, and three ears of corn. As he started a large wedge of chocolate cake, Kate remembered that they hadn't eaten breakfast.

Roberto grinned at Anders. "I notice you have a small appetite."

"Good food!" Anders exclaimed. "Do you always eat this way?"

"We've got the best cook in the business," Roberto said proudly. "Men leave other shows to work here because of our meals. That's why it's unusual when we're shorthanded."

He said no more until Anders finished his cake. Then Roberto asked, "Is there something I can do for you?"

"Well, now that you mention it—" Anders glanced sideways at Kate, and grinned. "I've always wanted to be a clown in a circus—a clown walking on stilts."

"You know how?" Roberto asked, obviously surprised.

"Yup!" Anders told him. "That man who got hurt—a boy said he's a stiltwalker. Can I take his place today?"

"Well, judging by the way you handled those horses, I'd say yes. Let's ask Slim if you can borrow his Uncle Sam costume. All you'd have to do is walk around and smile and wave."

Soon Roberto stood up. "We better get going."

Again Kate sensed that the clown wanted to say more. In everything, the circus people seemed to know exactly what they were doing. Whatever it involved, they did it well. For that reason, it seemed even stranger to have two accidents in a few hours.

"One more thing," Anders said as they left the cookhouse tent. "My sister Kate. Can she be a clown too?"

Me? Kate thought, as surprised by the request as Roberto

seemed to be. She had no doubt that anyone who was a clown worked hard to get there. But if there were some way to help Roberto, she wanted to try.

Roberto turned to Kate. "Well, that's a bit harder, but I'll think of something. By the way, did your family come along? I want to make sure they get front-row seats."

When they reached the dressing tent, Roberto gave Sarah reserved tickets for everyone in the family. She and M.R. left to find Mama and Papa.

Kate wasn't surprised when Roberto led her and Anders to an open area away from everyone.

"You wanted to tell me something?" he asked Anders.

The tall boy nodded. "On the runs this morning. Just before that bandwagon started rolling, the man on the flatcar—"

"The snubber, you mean?" Roberto asked. "He puts loops of rope around the snubbing post to keep the wagon from rolling down too fast."

"The snubber," Anders said. "He looked in your direction. Then he handled the rope a different way. Different from what he did for other wagons."

"That so?" Roberto's eyes were alert, as if he didn't want to miss a word.

"He let the rope out faster—too fast."

"You weren't imagining things?"

"I don't imagine things," Anders told him. He grinned, tipped his head toward Kate. "Now, *she* might. Kate has a good imagination."

Anders turned serious again. "But Kate notices things. That's why I asked if she could be a clown."

Anders looked Roberto straight in the eyes. "About the snubber. If the man with the chock block hadn't been there—"

Roberto nodded, and Kate knew he understood the warning. "I was busy keeping back the crowd," he said. "Usually I notice who's working as snubber. Did you see his face?"

As Kate described the man, Roberto looked puzzled. "A beard, you say? We're supposed to shave for the parade. And we always have a good man at the snubbing post."

Roberto ran his fingers through his hair. "We never have a bit of trouble when he's working. If the usual man wasn't there, who was? Would you describe him again?"

Finally Roberto shook his head. "It must be someone just hired. I thought it might be someone else."

"Someone else?" Anders asked.

Roberto's face was grim. "I wondered if it could be my enemy."

10

Puzzling Secrets

$\mathcal{R}$oberto clenched his fists. "There's a man who doesn't like me. In fact, he hates me. He does everything he can to get even."

As if with an effort, Roberto unclenched his hands, straightened his fingers. "Maybe it's not so strange, after all. Maybe that snubber *is* my enemy."

Instead of explaining what he meant, Roberto looked at Anders. "What happened in the parade wasn't an accident either. You were right about the wagon."

Roberto stood up, walked restlessly up and down. "Someone had unhooked the brake chain. Whoever it was knew we wouldn't need the brake until that hill. He also fixed the chain on the drag shoe so it would break at the worst possible place."

Kate longed to know more, but Roberto pulled out a pocket watch.

"I'll get you an outfit," he told Anders.

"And Kate?" her brother asked.

"I'll ask Linette."

"Linette?" Kate wondered aloud.

"My wife. She's an aerialist—flies from a trapeze. One of the best in the business. She'll know how to fix you up."

When Roberto led Anders into the men's dressing tent, Kate took a quick walk around the backyard. In a large horse top—a tent just for horses—Percherons drank water from canvas troughs. Nearby, blacksmiths worked, repairing harness.

As Kate returned to the dressing tent, she saw a high wire stretched between two poles. Wearing soft slipper shoes, tight-rope artists walked the length of the wire, warming up for their act.

Then Anders came out of the tent, dressed in red and white striped pants that were far too long for him. He had rolled up the pant legs to keep from walking on them.

In front, his blue coat came to the waist, then dropped down to tails in the back. On his head Anders wore a tall hat, again red and white striped, with a blue band of white stars around the crown.

Anders dropped down to a trunk standing on end. Roberto helped him wrap padding around his legs, then strap on the stilts. Instead of the straight poles Anders had used at home, these stilts had a short wooden base that served as a foot. A shoe covered each "foot."

When Anders stood up, his pant legs were just the right length. Even though Kate had seen her brother on stilts before, she wasn't prepared for his enormous height.

As she looked up at him, she laughed. "You must be twice as tall as I am!"

Anders grinned. "Two and a half feet taller than Big Gust!" The seven-foot six-inch giant was village marshall in Grantsburg, a town near Windy Hill Farm.

Anders walked around, getting used to the different kind of stilts. As he practiced, Linette returned. The pretty woman seemed quite a bit younger than Roberto.

"Troubles is really sick," Linette said when she heard Roberto's request. "It's the first time I've seen him too sick to work."

Linette explained to Kate. "Troubles, the clown. He's so short, you could wear his costume."

In the women's side of the dressing tent, Linette helped Kate.

"A pillow here, some padding there. We'll have you fixed up in no time." With thin pieces of rope she tied Kate together.

"A little more padding," she said finally. "Right on your behind."

When Kate pulled the clown costume over the padding, Linette exclaimed, "Perfect! Absolutely perfect!"

But Kate looked in the mirror and groaned. "I've gained at least thirty pounds!"

"Isn't that great? I've never done this before. You're the same size as Troubles!"

Once more she studied Kate. "Roberto gave me some makeup, so let me do your face."

"But I look awful!" Kate wailed. "What will M.R. think? He'll never want to be seen with me again!"

Linette drew back. For the first time she seemed to realize that Kate really disliked her appearance.

"Ahh, the boyfriend! Roberto told me, but I forgot about him. Don't you worry, honey. He'll never even know who you are!"

"I hope you're right," Kate said. "It might be the end of our friendship!"

"No, no!" Linette held up her hands. "Not if he's like Roberto. He'll understand."

Quickly she went to work, her hands sure and steady. She pulled back the hair around Kate's face. Then she wound Kate's long braid on top of her head. Next she covered the clown costume with a protective cloth.

Working swiftly, Linette smoothed white greasepaint onto Kate's face and neck. Once the skin was covered, Linette patted it all over, then added powder. When that had set, Linette removed any extra powder. She drew narrow eyebrows, triangles below Kate's eyes, and round red circles on her cheeks, nose, and chin.

As Kate watched in the mirror, she giggled. She was starting to feel better. Maybe Linette was right. Maybe M.R. wouldn't recognize her. She could hardly recognize herself!

"How do you know how to do this?" Kate asked.

"When Roberto fell from the rigging, he had a lot of injuries.

One of them was to his right arm," Linette said.

"What's the rigging?" Kate asked.

"The equipment used by trapeze artists. You know, the platforms, trapezes, everything they need."

Linette straightened. "Roberto and I worked together in a really big circus. He did all kinds of stunts most of us can't do. We were billed as the greatest flying act in the world."

"Is that why people call him the Great Roberto?" Kate asked.

Linette nodded. "People never stopped calling him that. We all know that even though Roberto can't do the act anymore, he's still great. He's great in other ways too—by the kind of person he is."

Linette painted a small mouth over Kate's lips. "After Roberto's accident, he became a clown. When his arm was still sore, I did his makeup for him."

At last Linette stood back. "Ahh! It is perfect!"

A curly red wig and a floppy hat covered Kate's braid. A large ruffled collar framed her face. Even Kate felt satisfied with the effect Linette had created.

"Now," she said briskly. "I'll introduce you to Mitsy."

Mitsy was a small black and white dog, a fox terrier, that surprised Kate with her friendliness.

"You just get to know her," Linette said. "Then Roberto will show you what to do."

Kate knelt down on the ground, held out her hand. When the dog came, Kate petted her, then scratched behind her ears. She kept talking until Mitsy knew her voice.

When Kate went back to Roberto, he stood outside the men's half of the dressing tent. The clown told Kate to fill her pockets with treats. Each time Mitsy did a trick, Kate should slip her something.

Roberto had watched Troubles enough to lead Kate through the tricks that Mitsy knew. More than once, as Kate spoke to her, the little dog cocked her head. She seemed unsure about what to do.

"Make your voice strong," Roberto told Kate.

"As though you're calling Lutfisk," Anders said. He was still walking around the yard, practicing on the stilts.

Kate changed the tone of her voice, trying to sound as if she knew exactly what she expected. This time the little dog obeyed Kate's commands.

"You've got it!" Roberto said at last. "Go through the tricks in that order, and you'll be all right."

The canvas side of the dressing tent was down now. In the heat of the day, Roberto had pulled his trunk outside. He shrugged into a suitcoat of large yellow and black checks.

"Mitsy knows a trick I don't want you to try," he told Kate. "She climbs a tall ladder, balances there, and then jumps off. Troubles catches her in his arms."

"You don't have to worry about that!" Kate exclaimed. "I'd be scared I'd drop her!"

"But just remember," Roberto warned. "Mitsy is used to that in the routine. She might do something you don't expect."

As the time for the show drew near, Kate heard band music from the Big Top. Outwardly Roberto looked calm. Yet underneath he seemed tense, and Kate suspected that she knew why.

More than once, during lunch she had noticed circus people drawn together in quiet huddles. Though she couldn't hear their whispers, Kate thought she knew their question. She, too, was wondering, *What's going to happen next?*

Only one day, she thought. *One day to find and catch whoever is trying to hurt Roberto.*

"I'm sorry you can't be an aerialist anymore," Kate told the clown. "But Linette says you're still the Great Roberto."

Roberto's brown eyes looked surprised. Then he smiled.

"I think she's right," Kate said softly. "You could be bitter and angry. It doesn't seem as if you are."

"You *do* notice things, don't you?" Roberto asked. "I *was* bitter at first, after the accident. It ate away at me."

"What happened?" Kate asked.

"I decided I could choose."

"Choose?" It was the word Papa had used when talking about marriage.

"Choose to waste whatever life I had left, or choose to do

something with it. People think I've come down in the world, going with a smaller circus as a clown. In a way I have. But I have a good job here. It's a circus I believe in."

Roberto stood up, his movements jerky with anger. "That's why I get upset when someone tries to wreck its good name. This circus is known as a Sunday school show. I want to keep it that way."

"What do you mean?" This time it was Anders who asked.

"Some circuses have a bad reputation. The management allows their ticket sellers to cheat people. They let pickpockets work the crowd. They figure, 'Well, we're going on to the next town. What does it matter? Let's grab whatever we can.' But the best shows—like the one I came from, and this one—they protect customers. They want a circus where families can come and have a good time."

Just then Linette came around from the women's side of the dressing tent. Walking quickly, she headed their way. When she caught sight of Kate and Anders, she stopped and waited for Roberto to go to her.

For a moment she smiled up at him. Their hands met, as in a warm clasp. Then she turned and ran quickly back in the direction from which she came.

Roberto slipped his hand into his pants pocket. His gaze followed Linette until she disappeared.

Then he started back to Kate and Anders. "That's our cue," he said. "Music for the come-in."

He looked over Kate's makeup. "Good, good! Your best friend won't recognize you!"

I hope not! Kate thought as Roberto checked the straps on the stilts Anders wore.

"You two go ahead," Roberto said finally. "Wait for me near the door of the Big Top."

They had almost reached the huge tent when Kate looked back. Roberto stood next to his open trunk. Kate couldn't quite see what he was doing, but he seemed to open a small drawer. Quickly he slipped his hand into his pocket, then into his trunk.

At this distance Kate couldn't be certain. Yet she felt sure

Roberto had concealed something inside his trunk. Something Linette had given him.

It bothered Kate. Yet when she said something to Anders, he answered, "Aw, Kate, this time you're imagining things."

In spite of her brother's words, Kate knew she was right. What were Linette and Roberto trying to hide?

11

Overheard Threats

*W*hen the clowns entered the Big Top for their walk-around, people were still finding their seats. Boys strolled up and down, selling popcorn and peanuts. Kate and Anders followed a clown who tumbled his way onto the dirt track that circled the three big rings.

Little children poked their parents and pointed toward Anders on his tall stilts. He pulled off his hat and bowed. When people cheered, he took great, long steps, then pretended he was going to fall. Instead, he caught himself and continued walking around the outer track.

Often Anders doubled back, as though to help Kate. People laughed when they saw the tall clown next to the little dog. Mitsy knew how she should act, and Kate had little to do but to follow her.

Soon Anders headed for the front row, and Kate wondered what her brother would try next. Then she spied Mama and Papa with Tina, Lars, and Darren. Sarah and M.R. had joined them too.

Oooops! Kate thought as she looked toward M.R. But he was watching Anders, not her, and Kate felt relieved. Yet she knew by the way her mother smiled that she hadn't been fooled.

When Anders reached the family, he leaned forward, grabbed Tina under her arms, and lifted her high. The crowd gasped, as though expecting the little girl to be afraid. Instead, Tina clung to her brother and giggled.

"Wow! Look at that!" someone shouted.

Anders set Tina on one shoulder and walked along the track. Whenever Tina waved, the crowd cheered. Finally Anders returned her to Mama and Papa. This time Anders held his hand to his ear until the audience clapped for him.

As he and Kate reached the performers' exit, a brassy fanfare broke into the buzz of excitement. Near the back wall of the Big Top, Kate and Anders stepped aside to watch.

Mounted riders carrying red, white, and blue flags burst through the door for the grand entry. A pretty girl rode the head of a swaying elephant, followed by a band playing a march.

With acrobats, jugglers, and tumblers all doing their part, the story of Cinderella unfolded. Ponies pulled Cinderella's lovely coach. Girls on dappled-gray horses followed close behind.

As the first performers finished circling the track, the rest of the elephants entered the tent. On the back of the last elephant stood Cinderella's prince!

By now the band had taken its place in the bandstand. While the elephants finished their shuffling walk, the music reached a crashing finale.

The ringmaster dashed forward. "Ladies and gentlemen! Boys and girls!" he called out, welcoming everyone to the circus. His high black boots, white pants, and red coat drew the gaze of the crowd.

With outstretched arm, the ringmaster pointed to the large cage filling the center ring. "I call your attention to the most amazing, death-defying act you'll ever see. Before your eyes, lions and tigers—natural enemies in the wild! Here, today, you will see these big cats *together* in the same cage!

"I present to you the most daring wild animal trainer on earth—the one, the only Tyrone!"

To the roll of drums a worker lifted the first gate in the cage wagons placed end to end. As the lion trainer waited in the large center cage, a lion raced through the chute into the center ring.

Tyrone pointed his whip toward a pedestal. "Up! Up!" As the lion leaped to its place, a second lion bounded through the chute and took its pedestal.

The third lion paused as though refusing to go up. Tyrone stared at the lion and gave the order again. This time the animal leaped to its place.

The next arrival was a tiger, slinking its way into the cage. Another tiger followed the first.

"Up! Up!" the trainer ordered each big cat.

They're trained, Kate thought as she watched the tigers take their places between the lions. *Yet they're natural enemies. Enemies, too, of the man who tells them what to do.*

As the big cats waited on pedestals of different heights, Tyrone called them down for special tricks. One of the lions walked on its hind legs. A tiger balanced on a ball, and another leaped through a flaming hoop. Then the three lions lay down together with the trainer sitting among them.

Just one snap of the jaw! Only one wrong move—a great paw, a leaping body. Kate didn't like to think about it.

It seemed as though Papa had just finished reading about Daniel in the lions' den. What would happen if even one of these snarling cats went back to his jungle ways?

Before long, a tiger batted the air. He stretched out its paw as though to strike a lion. The lion bared its teeth and snarled.

Instantly the trainer cracked his whip in the air. "Down, Sheba," he commanded, as if he had no fear.

The lion stared at him, but waited.

"Down, Sheba!" the trainer commanded again. This time the big cat obeyed.

Kate didn't want the act to end. At the same time she felt relieved when one big cat after another bounded back through the cage wagons. The story of Daniel had never seemed so real.

———

Pony acts performed in the two end rings as men took down

the large cage in the center ring. Then aerial acrobats hung up-side down, held by ropes and trapezes far above the sawdust-covered earth.

As they finished their act, the ringmaster stepped forward. Roberto leaped from the audience. In his yellow and black suit, he walked boldly into the center ring.

"Who are you?" the ringmaster asked.

"The Great Roberto," the clown replied with dignity. Yet he sounded a bit tipsy. "From Hudson, Wisconsin."

The crowd laughed and broke into applause. Everyone knew that Hudson was a town near River Falls.

"Hudson, you say?" The ringmaster scratched his head.

"I've come to ride your best horse."

"Our best horse?" the ringmaster asked. "Certainly not! Why, he'd buck you right off!"

But Roberto insisted, and a huge black horse was brought out. Roberto tried to climb on from the wrong side, and the horse bucked.

The crowd gasped, but Roberto tried again. When he succeeded in getting onto the horse's back, he fell off on the other side.

The crowd laughed at his clumsiness, but a cold sense of warning hit Kate's stomach. Was it her imagination? Or had the saddle shifted just a bit? If so, the movement was so slight Roberto hadn't felt it.

Suddenly Anders stalked forward. "Wait! Wait!" he cried out, as though part of the act. "A new saddle for the gentleman from Hudson!"

Roberto stared at him, but Anders called again. "A new saddle for this gentleman rider!"

Before anyone could say another thing, Anders leaned down and unbuckled the strap around the horse's belly. When a worker ran in with another saddle, Anders waited until the new saddle was in place.

The moment Roberto jumped onto the black horse, it raced off. Roberto slipped to one side, hanging down as though ready to fall off.

"What was wrong?" Kate asked as Anders returned to her.

"The girth—the strap under the horse's belly. Someone tampered with it."

"So it would break?"

Anders nodded. "At just the right time—or wrong time, I should say."

Kate tried to push away her fear. Yet it washed over like waves. "Anders, I'm so scared. What's going to happen next?"

Her brother shrugged. "That's just what someone wants us to wonder."

He looked back toward Roberto. Around the track the horse galloped. The clown's head hung only a few inches above the flying hooves.

Then Roberto straightened, pulled himself up, and started showing his riding skill. The audience roared in approval as they realized they had been fooled.

After that, other acts followed in quick succession. Acrobats, high wire artists, and bareback riders filled the rings.

Between acts, Kate and Anders again circled the track with other clowns. This time Kate followed Roberto, who now wore whiteface makeup. A pointed cap rested on top of his orange wig. With a big smiling mouth and a polka-dot clown costume, he strolled along in large floppy shoes.

While Kate walked with Mitsy, Anders stayed nearby, holding out a long stiffened rope. Each time he hurried ahead, as though an invisible dog pulled him along, the crowd burst into laughter.

———

As the show neared its end, Kate once more stood near the back door where performers came in and out. From there Kate had a good view of the aerial act.

Two high platforms stood on opposite sides of the center ring. A long net stretched below and between the platforms. Above that were the swings used by the trapeze artists.

Linette posed on one of the small platforms. Next to her was Alex of the Flying Alden Brothers. Across the large open space,

Will sat on a trapeze, as much at ease as on a backyard swing.

In a bright red costume Linette waited, holding a rose out over the edge of the platform. When she had the crowd's attention, she let the flower go.

As it fell to the ground far below, Kate knew what Linette was saying. *It's a long way down.* The fear Kate already felt threatened to overwhelm her. *What if there's another accident?*

Then Will pushed an empty trapeze toward Linette and Alex. Catching hold, Alex leaped out. Linette followed on a different trapeze. Far above center ring, she hung with her hands on the bar, swinging back and forth.

"Is it hard for you to watch her?" Kate whispered to Roberto as Linette leaped back onto the platform.

"Sometimes." The clown had joined Kate as the flying act began. "Their timing has to be perfect."

On the next swing, Alex moved in wider and wider arcs, then somersaulted toward Will. As Will caught him by the wrists, Alex flipped around and returned to his trapeze.

As the act increased in difficulty, Alex passed Linette in the air. Once more they returned to the starting platform.

There Linette caught her trapeze, swung it toward Will. As he returned it, Will clapped his hands. Linette caught the bar. Flying between the two men, she did a double somersault.

"There aren't many who can do a double," Roberto said as applause filled the tent.

Linette returned to her starting platform. On his platform across the way, Will stood on tiptoe, trapeze in hand. His lips moved as he counted.

Suddenly he leaped into the air, swung high, and twisted upside down. With his knees wrapped around the ropes of his trapeze, he caught Linette on a return swing.

During the next arc of the trapeze, Will tossed her to Alex, then passed above them. Instantly Alex flipped Linette above his head. As she streaked through the air, Will caught her. The crowd gasped.

At the end of the act, Linette swung to the center of the rigging and dropped into the safety net. Alex followed with a quick somersault on the way down.

But Will flew out on his trapeze, swinging high toward the canvas ceiling. When he left the bar, he dropped in a swan dive. Just before reaching the net, he flipped up, landed with his feet, and bounced high.

Once more he dropped. This time he swung from the net to the ground.

Linette and the men ran forward to take their bows. The audience thundered its applause.

As Linette ran gracefully toward the exit, Kate sighed. She wondered how long she had held her breath.

"That's what you used to do?" she asked Roberto.

He nodded. "We made a good team."

Moments later, all of the acts spilled through the back door for the grand finale. Kate fell into line behind Anders and Roberto to march around the track. As Kate completed the circle, she heard the cry of the ringmaster. "May all your days be circus days!"

When the audience poured out through the other exits, Kate stayed near the door to the backyard, watching them go. She hated to see the excitement and sparkle end.

Though still afternoon, it had been a long day—up before dawn, then the excitement of all that had gone wrong. Kate started to lean against the wall, then remembered it was canvas.

It didn't seem possible that anything more could happen. Yet Kate was starting to feel jumpy about everything. Where could a person who wanted to cause trouble strike next?

If only we could outguess him—figure out what he's going to do. Maybe we could prevent an accident.

Just then Kate heard voices from the other side of the canvas wall.

"He gets all the breaks," a man's voice said.

"What do you mean, all the breaks?" a woman asked.

"Everything comes easy for him."

"That's not true," the woman answered. Her voice sounded familiar. "He's worked hard for everything he has, including his reputation."

Kate stiffened. Who were they talking about?

The man's laugh sounded harsh. "Well, he beat me out with you. But it won't happen with anything else."

"What do you mean?" The woman's voice sounded sharp.

"Just that. I'll get what I want."

Kate trembled, but the woman laughed.

It's Linette! Kate thought. The aerialist sounded as if she were trying to hide her fear.

"Well, good luck! It didn't work before, and it won't work now!"

"So?" The angry mutter sounded like a growl. "No one—not even Roberto—is going to stop me this time!"

Again Kate trembled. Who was the man? He, too, sounded familiar. If Kate could find out who it was, she might know who caused the mysterious accidents.

"No one?" Linette asked. "I'm going to tell Roberto you're here!"

Moving soundlessly, Kate ran to the door. Like a shadow, she slipped into the sunlight. As she doubled back toward the place where she heard the voices, she bent down to pass beneath one guide rope, then another. Finally she rounded a corner of the tent.

Linette was nowhere in sight. Whoever had been there was gone.

12

Master of Disguises

*W*hy? Kate wondered as she hurried away from the Big Top. *Who tried to threaten Linette?* Though the voice Kate had heard seemed familiar, she couldn't place it.

Questions spun around in her mind. But when Kate entered the women's side of the dressing tent, Linette was nowhere in sight.

Only one day to solve the mystery, Kate thought, as she had before. *And that day is two-thirds over.* She was beginning to feel desperate.

In the midsummer heat, hot air seemed to rise in waves from the ground. With a knot in her stomach, Kate started around to the men's side of the tent. Just then Roberto entered the backyard. In his polka clown costume, he hurried over to her flat-topped trunk.

Kate stopped, realizing the clown had not seen her. Had Linette found him? Kate didn't think there had been enough time. Yet Roberto seemed upset. As he sat down on a bench, he opened the trunk.

Starting forward again, Kate came up behind him. From this view she could look into the trunk. On the inside of the top cover was a mirror. By tipping back the lid, Roberto had a ready-made dressing table.

The bottom half of the trunk was filled with clothes. Kate saw another costume just like the polka dot one that Roberto wore. While Kate paused, wondering what to say, he pushed aside the clothing.

Small drawers were built along one side. As Roberto started to open one of the drawers, he glanced up and around. Suddenly he saw Kate behind him.

"Can I do something for you?" he asked. With a quick movement he pushed the clothing back over the drawers.

Kate felt a warm flush creep into her cheeks. She had been caught spying.

"Did Linette find you?" Kate asked quickly, trying to cover her embarrassment.

Roberto shook his head. "I've been talking to the boss." He reached out, closed the trunk cover.

As it slammed down, Kate almost lost her courage. Yet when Roberto sat still, waiting, she had to say something.

"The man who hates you. Does he want to get even with you?"

Roberto's injured right arm jerked, as though he felt nervous. Yet his large painted smile remained steady as he nodded yes.

"Is he someone who would threaten Linette?" Kate asked.

Roberto's makeup hid his true thoughts, but his dark brown eyes looked uneasy. "Why do you want to know?"

I like Roberto, Kate thought. At the start she had trusted him. But then she saw Linette pass something to him. Again Kate wondered, *What are they trying to hide?*

As Kate stood there, her gaze met Roberto's. *Sarah likes him. Does that mean I can trust him?*

"Kate, if there's something wrong, I need to know."

Roberto's voice was quiet and even sad. Yet Kate recognized the way in which he spoke. She'd seen that same kind of strength in Papa Nordstrom and other people she trusted. For some strange reason she thought of Erik and wished he were here.

Stumbling over the words, Kate started to tell the clown about the man outside the Big Top. Partway through, Kate got caught up in the story, and all that she had heard tumbled out.

Only once did Roberto interrupt her, asking a question. But when Kate finished, it was as though the clown spit bad food from his mouth. "He's back!"

"Who's back?" Kate asked.

"The man who ruined my life. He messed with the rigging, so I fell."

Roberto jumped up. "With all that's gone wrong, I was sure he had followed us again."

Roberto hurried to the door leading into the tent with animal cages. "Wait here," he told Kate, then disappeared.

By the time Roberto returned, Kate had more questions. "Why does that man hate you?"

"We both worked for a different circus," Roberto said. "He made good money, but got greedy and wanted more. Between shows, he mixed with the crowds, picking pockets."

"Stealing from people who came to the circus?"

Roberto nodded. "When I figured out what he was doing, I told him to stop. He was ruining the good name of our circus."

"And he didn't like what you said?"

"Said I should mind my own business. When I told him I'd go to the boss, he started making trouble, even with Linette."

"Why Linette?"

"He wanted to marry her. When she wouldn't have anything to do with him, he blamed it on me. One night he messed with the rigging."

"But how?" Kate asked.

"He knew just what to do to make things look right, but have them unsafe," Roberto said. "That's how he tricked me."

"And you fell?"

Roberto nodded. "I could have been killed. As it was, it wrecked my career. I can't be a catcher without strong arms. I could drop someone."

The clown sighed. "We couldn't prove it, of course. It looked as if someone had been careless. But that's how he got a bad name. He lost his job because no one wanted to work with him."

The more Kate heard, the more concerned she felt. "Would he hurt Linette?"

Roberto put his hand to his head as though to run his fingers through his hair. Instead, he felt the orange wig. As he lowered his hand, it trembled.

"I'm sorry," Kate said.

"When Linette and I worked together, we always had a good time. But she didn't want to marry me. When I got hurt, I was angry at the man who caused the accident. But after I sorted things out—moved beyond being angry and bitter—why then, Linette wanted to be my wife!"

Roberto's voice was filled with emotion, as if, even yet, he felt surprised that Linette would marry him.

With all her heart Kate wished she could say, "Linette will be all right. She's not in danger."

Yet Kate knew that she couldn't. Too much had already happened. No one knew where trouble would strike next.

"Does someone check the rigging between performances?" Kate asked. "To make sure that it's safe?"

Roberto nodded, but looked tired and old with worry. "Just the same, I'll make sure there's someone there every minute. Then I'll find Linette."

Again Roberto stood up. "We've got some time. Why don't you look around and see the rest of the circus? Then I'll take you to the cookhouse for supper."

As Roberto hurried across the grass to the Big Top, he limped as though his entire body hurt. It reminded Kate of the accident that should not have happened.

Watching him, Kake realized something and started after him. "Roberto, who *is* this man?" she called as she tried to catch up.

In that moment Linette appeared. "He's back!" she exclaimed. Her pretty face was flushed with anger.

"Where were you?" she asked Roberto. "I tried to find you!" Linette's voice broke as if she couldn't handle anything more. She began to cry.

Roberto hurried to her, put his arms around her. "It'll be all right," he said. "I'll take care of you."

Linette's shoulders shook with sobs. Finally she drew a long breath. "Leo threatened me!"

"Leo?" Kate asked. "That's why his voice sounded familiar! He put up posters in Frederic."

Roberto nodded. "I checked with the man who hires workers. He fired Leo because of the way he treated someone's dog."

"My brother's," Kate said.

"Leo's going to hurt you!" Linette told Roberto. "He said that not even you can stop him this time!"

"When Kate told me what happened, I talked to the boss again," Roberto said. "We're doing everything we can to find Leo."

"But I don't understand." Kate felt puzzled. "I thought the man causing trouble would be the snubber."

"Maybe it is." Roberto sounded tired and angry at the same time.

"What do you mean?" Kate asked.

"It seems that Leo lied about his name. He changed his looks and managed to get hired again, here in River Falls. The boss has every circus worker looking for him."

Roberto sighed. "But there's a big problem." He shook his head as though finding it hard to believe himself. "Leo is a master of disguises. We never know what he'll look like next."

13

The Lion's Den

*I*n the women's side of the dressing tent, Kate patted oil on her face. With a towel she wiped off her makeup, then changed out of her clown costume.

She found Sarah and M.R. near the red wagon for selling tickets. Tina and Mama and baby Bernie waited with them.

By now Bernie was tired and fussy. As Mama tried to soothe him, his little body stiffened, as though his stomach hurt.

"I'll walk back to the house," Mama said. "He'll settle down where it's more quiet." She asked Tina to come along.

"I want to see the animals," Tina wailed, sounding almost as tired as the baby. "I want to see the big kitties."

Mama looked apologetic. "When we went into the tent with animal cages, it was so crowded, Papa had to hold her up. Even so, she couldn't see very well."

"I'll take her," Kate said quickly. "We'll show her the animals, then bring her to you."

"Thanks, Kate." Mama looked relieved.

Kate held out her hand to Tina. The little girl tugged one of her pigtails.

"C'mon, Tina," Kate said. "I haven't seen the animals either.

Let's go find the hippopotamus."

M.R. walked with Kate and Tina to the tent with animal cages. Sarah and Anders trailed close behind.

"I didn't see you in the circus," M.R. told Kate.

"Oh, you didn't?" Kate asked, pretending surprise. "I walked around the dirt track."

"I was really watching," he said. "What were you wearing?"

As Kate tried to think what to say, Anders jumped in. "It was a very becoming costume!"

"It was?" Sarah asked. "I didn't see you either, Kate. Were you really out there?"

"You betcha, she was out there!" Anders exclaimed. "Best act in the circus!"

He looked at Kate. "Maybe if you describe your costume better—"

Kate glared at him and quickly leaned down to talk to Tina. She was speaking more English now than when Kate first came to Windy Hill Farm.

Guards stood near the cage wagons to make sure that no one bothered the animals. Curious people still walked up and down, but there was room for Tina to see.

The huge elephants stood at a picket line. The chain stretched from one strong stake to another. Other chains, attached to the main one, circled a rear leg on each elephant.

As Kate watched, a gigantic bull snuffled the ground. Raising his trunk, he sprayed dirt over his back. Another elephant curled his trunk around a bunch of hay and dropped it into his mouth. Lars and Darren were there, bringing water.

For Kate it was exciting to watch the animals. While she had seen pictures of such wild beasts, she had never been closer to them than in a parade.

She and M.R. took Tina from wagon to wagon. When they came to the hippopotamus, Anders held the little girl up. The cage had a large water tank. The hippo lay within it, its body half covered by water.

Nearby, a large male lion paced back and forth behind bars,

as though waiting to be fed. His huge mane seemed to frame his face.

"There's a mother lion with two cubs in the backyard," Kate told Tina. "She's there to be away from the crowd. If you're quiet, I'll ask if you can see her."

When a guard Kate had met gave permission, she led the others into the backyard. A short distance from the canvas wall of the tent for animals, a cage wagon stood by itself. With iron bars on both sides, it had a wooden wall on each end.

Inside the cage, the mother lion licked her cubs. As Kate and Tina walked close, the mother raised her head and looked them over. The cubs snuggled closer.

"Pretty kitty," Tina said. Her white-blond hair curled around the edge of her face. She laid down her doll on the pole of the wagon, safely away from the dirt of the circus lot.

"Nice kitty." Tina reached out her hand as if to pet the lion.

"No," Kate said sharply. "Keep your hands back. She's not like the kittens you have at home."

For a while Tina stood there, watching. Finally she looked up at Kate. "This is the *best* part of the circus!"

Kate smiled, glad that Tina also liked the animals. But M.R. was growing impatient.

"Let's go get some lemonade," he said.

Kate held back, and M.R. guessed she was wondering about money. "My treat," he said.

Kate and the others followed him through the tent with animal cages. On the far side, they came to the large cloth banners that advertised the sideshow.

People still filled the sawdust pathway. While walking to the lemonade tent, Kate told the others what she had learned.

"A master of disguises?" Sarah asked, her brown eyes wide. "Then how can you possibly find him? You'll never know what he looks like!"

"That's what Roberto said." Kate fought down the scared feelings that threatened to overwhelm her.

"Kate, I don't think you should be mixed up in this," M.R. said. "You could really get hurt."

"I'll be careful," Kate promised. "We've faced hard things before." She glanced at Anders, but even her brother looked worried.

A crowd of people waited in front of the tent that sold lemonade. As M.R. and Anders stepped into line, Sarah told them they'd wait in the shade of a tree.

"Get a lemonade for Tina too," she called after them.

"Tina!" In that instant Kate remembered the five-year-old. She had been right behind them as they passed through the tent with animal cages. "Where is she?"

Kate whirled around, staring back in the direction from which they'd come. People of all sizes and shapes packed the walkway.

Filled with panic, Kate started back in the direction from which they came. As she hurried past the banners, they seemed a blur. "Tina! Tina!" Kate called.

People in the crowd turned to look. When Kate broke into a run, they stepped aside, making way. But there was no sign of the little girl.

In the tent with cage wagons, Kate passed the bears and tigers, then the hippo den.

"Tina!" she cried again, the terror within her growing. When she reached the cage at the far end, Kate stopped so suddenly she almost fell over. Looking around, she tried to decide what to do.

Then she remembered the mother lion. *Tina wanted to pet her!* Quickly Kate slipped through the door into the backyard.

To her relief, she saw the five-year-old near the lion cage. As Kate hurried that way, Tina picked up her doll from the pole at the front of the wagon. With Annabelle in her arms, Tina moved closer to the iron bars.

The mother lion stood with her two cubs brushing against her legs. Eyeing Tina, the lioness growled low in her throat, then circled her cubs. Sniffing with each step, she padded to the wooden end of the cage.

What's wrong? Kate wondered. Only minutes before, the lioness had been resting, enjoying her cubs. Now she seemed to be protecting them.

At the closed-in wall the lioness sniffed again. As though bothered by something she couldn't see, she lifted her head and roared. Turning, she threw herself against the bars of the cage.

Tina leaped back, looking frightened. As Kate reached the little girl, the big cat bared her teeth and snarled. Again she circled her cubs.

What's bothering her? Kate wondered once more. Then, at the end of the cage, she caught a quick movement. A man stood behind the wooden wall with only his legs showing between the wheels.

In the next moment, the lioness became frantic. Once, twice, three times, she threw herself against the bars.

Tina grabbed Kake's hand. Again the mother threw herself, this time against the door of the cage.

Under her weight, the bars moved. The door opened. The lioness leaped down!

As her large paws touched dirt, she raised her head and looked around. She was free!

Kate stepped in front of Tina. The quick movement caught the lion's attention. Fixing her gaze on Kate and Tina, she crouched, ready to spring.

14

Who? What? Where?

$\mathcal{F}$illed with terror, Kate felt as though she were rooted to the ground.

From the cage one of the cubs whined. For one instant the mother glanced back toward her young.

Slowly the lioness straightened. Without blinking, she stared at Kate and Tina. Then she lifted one great paw, set it down.

From behind, Kate felt Tina shift her feet. Kate turned her head. "Don't move," she whispered through stiff lips.

Yet her own knees wobbled. Then her entire body trembled. One thought whirled round and round. *What can I do?*

Again the lioness bared its teeth. Like a cat stalking a mouse, she started toward Kate and Tina.

Kate took one step backward. Behind her, Tina moved. From the other side of the canvas wall, a bird squawked. As though sensing something wrong, an elephant trumpeted.

The lioness stopped, then lifted another paw.

Overwhelmed by panic, Kate jerked back. Like a quick breath, a prayer spilled from her lips. "Help me, God. Help *us!*"

The lioness raised its head, as if listening. Only then did Kate realize she had spoken aloud.

In the next moment pictures seemed to flash before her eyes. Roberto teaching her how to talk to Mitsy. The animal trainer staring at the big cats.

With an effort Kate breathed deep. *The lion doesn't know me.*

Trying to push aside her panic, Kate struggled to remember. What had the animal trainer done? Whatever it was, he acted as though he wasn't afraid.

Kate faced the lion. "It's all right." She spoke through stiff lips, trying to sound calm. But her voice shook with fear.

Again she tried. "It's all right." This time she sounded stronger. Raising her voice, she spoke louder. "We won't hurt your cubs."

As though the mother understood, she tossed her head, looked around. One cub stood in the door of the cage, studying the distance to the ground.

Just then, beyond the lioness, Kate saw Sarah come through the back door of the tent. As Sarah stopped in her tracks, a man appeared behind her. An instant later, he disappeared.

A soft moan escaped Kate's lips. Didn't he see what was happening?

Once more, the mother lion fixed her gaze on Kate.

"It's all right." Kate spoke loudly, trying to sound like a schoolteacher. But her muscles knotted as she tried not to move.

Moments later, the circus worker stepped through the door from the cage wagons. With him was an armed man. Three other men held a long piece of canvas.

Quietly they edged forward, trying not to frighten the lioness. Yet as the canvas wall moved closer, she twitched her tail.

At the door of the cage the cub whimpered. Its mother looked back.

The men with the canvas closed in. From within the cage the other cub whimpered.

Again the mother turned toward the sound, as if wondering what to do.

Suddenly she crouched. With a quick spring, she leaped into the cage. One of the men bounded toward the cage and shut the door.

Without warning Kate's knees gave way. As she dropped to the ground, Tina fell into her arms. Kate clutched her, sobbing, as though she would never let the little girl go.

Then the circus men reached them. "You're all right?" the first one asked. Kate could only nod.

"Good thinking," said another. "Talking loud. Sounding calm. I heard your voice through the canvas."

Just the same, they, too, looked as shaken as Kate felt. When she looked up, she saw that Sarah was also crying.

A moment later, Linette was there, and Roberto. In spite of his large, smiling mouth, his eyes looked worried.

"What happened?" he asked.

"The latch on the cage wasn't closed," Kate said when she could speak. "When the lion jumped against it, it opened."

Roberto glanced around. "Someone just cleaned the cage?" he asked.

One of the men nodded. "Boys use a long-handled brush," he told Kate. "Stick the brush through the door."

He turned back to Roberto. "I'll check with all of 'em. If someone left the cage open, he's out of a job."

"Just a minute," Kate said. Something tugged at the back of her mind. Only minutes before, the mother had been licking her cubs. Why had she become frantic? Who was bothering her?

Kate struggled to think. Just before that terrible moment when the door opened, she had seen a man's legs at the end of the wagon. Had he unlocked the cage?

Kate looked toward the wagon, through the bars on the two sides of the cage. Whoever was there had slipped away. Like a shadow he had gone while she faced the lion. Yet he would have seen her need for help.

When Kate told Roberto, he asked quickly, "Can you describe him?"

Kate shook her head. "I saw only the bottom of his legs and his shoes."

Linette covered her mouth with her hands, but a frightened cry escaped her lips. "He said he'd get even!"

"Hush!" Roberto commanded. "It doesn't do any good to be

afraid. That's just what he wants."

"Someone is trying to ruin our circus," one of the men said.

"And *us*," Linette answered. "He's trying to ruin Roberto and me. To make it so awful that no one wants us to work in their circus."

Kate struggled to her feet. She still felt shaky, but there was something she had to know.

Slowly she circled the lion's cage, searching for any clue left by the man who had been there. Near the wagon pole she found half a peanut shell, but nothing else.

As Kate joined Roberto again, Anders and M.R. appeared. When they learned what had happened, they, too, were upset.

It was Linette who asked the question that all of them dreaded. "What will that terrible man do next?"

"I don't know," Roberto answered. "I talked to the boss. He told the police to keep a special watch. He's asking all the people in the circus to be on their guard."

"In just a few hours, the circus starts leaving town." Sarah's brown eyes looked worried.

"We don't have much time," Anders said. "If you go without finding Leo, will he follow you?"

"I'm afraid so," Roberto answered. "He's done it more than once. We never know where he is. We never guess what he's planning until he strikes again."

———

Kate, Anders, Sarah, and M.R. walked to Granny's, taking Tina to Mama. While there, Kate made certain that her face was good and clean.

As the four returned to the circus grounds, Anders and M.R. walked ahead. In spite of all that had happened, Kate still felt an invisible wall between her and Sarah.

She looks so pretty, Kate thought as Sarah pushed back her honey-blond hair. *So sure of herself. And this morning I looked so awful.* Kate felt embarrassed just remembering the ring of dirt M.R. had seen around her face.

Then Sarah asked, "Kate?"

She sounded as uncertain as Kate felt. For the first time, she wondered if Sarah really did feel shy. But that seemed hard to believe.

"You were so good with Darren," Sarah said. "How did you know what to say?"

Kate shrugged. "I guess I just understood the way he felt."

"But aren't you ever afraid?"

"Afraid?" The wall that Kate had built up seemed to have a crack in it.

"Being a clown, for instance. Weren't you scared?"

Kate grinned. "As Anders would say, 'You betcha!' Before I went out in front of all those people, I almost turned and ran!"

"But you didn't! And with the lion— Kate, you *talked* to the lion. How could you?"

Kate laughed nervously. "Oh, that was nothing!" She brushed it away. If she said more, she'd have to talk about God, and she wasn't going to do that. Sarah would tell M.R. for sure.

But then Kate fell silent. *How can I possibly say it was nothing?* For the rest of her life she would never forget that moment of facing the lion. The fear she felt, yes, but even more, what she had learned about God's help.

"I can't take credit for what I did," Kate said finally. Her voice was small and echoed her fear of what Sarah would think. For some strange reason that seemed almost as awful as facing the lion.

"Can't take credit?" The idea startled Sarah. "But who did it if you didn't?"

"God helped me," Kate said, her voice even smaller.

"Oh, Kate!" Sarah stared at her. "*Whatever* do you mean?"

Kate wished she could disappear into a hole in the ground. *No matter what I say, Sarah will think I'm strange.*

Before Kate could answer, Sarah hurried on. "You honestly think that a God, who no one ever sees, really helps you?"

"Yes, I do," Kate said quietly, but with a sureness that filled every part of her being. "God can."

"God *can*?" Sarah stopped in her tracks. "God can do what?"

Kate faced her. "God can help you. If you let Him, that is. If you ask for help."

"You really mean that, don't you?"

To Kate's surprise Sarah struggled to speak. "Oh, Kate, I get so scared. I was scared, even of you."

"Of *me*?" Kate couldn't believe what she heard. She was the one who had been scared of Sarah and the sure-of-herself way she looked.

"When you met us at the train, I could see right away that you had changed," Sarah said. "I thought it was because you have a new brother—a nice brother." Sarah's face grew pink, but Kate understood.

"Ever since you came, I've watched you," Sarah went on. "I've been afraid to be what I am. I was afraid—"

"Of what I'd think." Kate giggled, but her laughter was close to tears.

"How did you know?"

"'Cause that's how I felt about you!"

Right there, on the side of the road, Kate opened her arms and closed them around her friend. Sarah's arms tightened around Kate in a big hug.

"Let's start over," she said. As they walked along Cedar Street, Sarah told Kate about every friend she remembered.

When they neared the circus lot, the crowd was once again growing. Already people had come for the evening show. Near the entrance to the circus, steam billowed from the calliope. Kate hurried forward.

"What are you doing?" M.R. asked as he followed her.

Kate knocked on the door on the back side of the wagon. "Please," she said to the man inside. "Will you tell me about the whistles?"

"Thirty-two of 'em," he answered, and Kate climbed up on the step where she could see.

He showed Kate the long wires that led from the keyboard to the whistles. "When I push down a key, I open a valve. Steam shoots up through the whistle."

With strong-looking fingers, he touched the keyboard,

swung into "Billy Boy." At the end of a verse he stopped.

Kate spoke quickly. "Can I play it?"

"Sure can," the man answered. "But you've gotta plunk your fingers down mighty hard." He moved aside to give Kate room on the bench.

Kate did just as he told her. Yet no matter how hard she pushed the keys, they wouldn't go down. She did not have enough strength.

Filled with disappointment, she finally had to give up. *I wish Erik were here,* she thought for the first time since leaving home. *He would understand.*

Then M.R. held out his hand to help her down the step. When his smile flashed, Kate pushed all thought of Erik aside.

"I want to be a great organist someday," Kate told M.R. as they hurried on. It seemed important that he know the things that meant the most to her.

M.R. listened as he always did, but Kate wasn't sure he understood. "Why do you want to be a great organist?" he asked.

Kate started to explain, then stopped. If she told him the biggest reason, she'd have to explain what God meant in her life.

When they reached the backyard, Linette was waiting for them. "Roberto asked me to take you to supper," she said.

As soon as they finished eating, the aerialist led Kate to the women's side of the dressing tent. This time Kate tied on the padding herself.

Then Linette started to put on Kate's makeup. Her movements were jerky and nervous. The hand that had been so steady now trembled.

When Linette drew a wobbly line around Kate's mouth, she threw down the brush in despair. "In all the time I've been with the circus, I've never had such a day! Everything has gone wrong!"

She picked up another brush, tried again. When that line also looked wobbly, she gave up. "Oh, Kate, I just can't do it! I'm so jumpy. I just keep wondering, 'What's going to happen next?' "

"Maybe Leo is through making trouble for the day," Kate said.

But Linette hurried out of the tent, around to the other end. As Kate followed, Linette called out, "Roberto! Will you help Kate?"

The clown stood near his open trunk.

"It's gone!" he said.

"What's gone?" Linette asked.

"My extra polka-dot costume. It was here earlier today. Someone's been in my trunk."

15

The Runaway Clown

*R*oberto's clown costume ballooned around him. His big, laughing mouth looked strange when he was so upset.

Linette glanced toward Kate, then back to Roberto. Her face seemed to turn a shade whiter.

"But you aren't missing anything else." Linette spoke as though she knew the answer, but her voice sounded sharp with worry.

Roberto nodded in agreement. For a moment their gaze held.

They're still hiding something, Kate thought. *What is it? Why don't they trust me with knowing?*

Before she had more time to think about it, Roberto sat down on a trunk and began making up Kate's face.

"I stayed in the Big Top all through supper," he told Linette. His voice sounded steady and confident, as though he wanted to calm her. "Another man is there now, and he'll stay as long as we need him."

Linette tried to smile. "I'll go warm up," she said.

Roberto worked quickly on Kate's makeup. "You were great with Mitsy," he said, as though nothing had happened since the afternoon show. "She acted as if she'd known you all her life."

Kate wanted to smile and say thank you, but she couldn't move her lips while Roberto was putting on the makeup.

"Dogs know human nature," Roberto went on. "It's like an instinct with them. Mitsy's well trained, but I don't think she'd do her tricks if she didn't like you."

As Roberto put the final touch on Kate's makeup, a man hurried around the corner of the tent. His clothes were wet with sweat from the heat of the afternoon. His face told Kate that something more was wrong.

The man glanced at Kate, then back at Roberto.

"It's all right," Roberto said quickly. "Kate is helping us."

"There's a pickpocket working the crowd," the man said.

"Do you know who it is?" Roberto asked, as if he weren't surprised.

"I didn't see him." The circus worker stepped closer to Roberto and lowered his voice. "Linette talked to me. She said that a man named Leo is here. From what she said, it sounds like his work."

Roberto nodded. "Have you told anyone else?"

"I'll find the boss, but I wanted to warn you first. Be careful, Roberto. You and Linette mean a lot to me. We don't want anything more going wrong."

As quickly as the man came, he disappeared around the tent.

"Wait a minute!" Roberto called. "I'll go with you. I want to talk to the boss myself."

When Roberto left, Kate found Mitsy. As she led the little dog through her tricks, M.R. and Sarah appeared.

Seeing M.R., Kate edged back, trying to get away.

M.R. stared at her. "Kate?"

When she didn't answer, he started to laugh. "It's really you! I missed it completely the first time."

Kate cringed, wished she could pull off the red wig.

But M.R. laughed again. "I can't believe you fooled me! I guess I was looking for your black hair. Where did you learn to act so well?"

Sarah thought the best part of the joke was having M.R.

fooled. She sat down on a trunk and watched Kate with Mitsy.

Just then Linette appeared, dressed in the costume she wore for her act. "Where's Roberto?" she asked.

"He went to talk to someone he calls the boss," Kate said.

A frown crossed Linette's pretty face. "Sarah, could you do something for me? Wait until Roberto gets back and give him this?"

As Sarah nodded, Linette slipped her a small cloth bag. "Be very careful with it," she warned.

That's what she passes to Roberto before her act, Kate thought. She felt sure that Linette tied the small bag to a chain around her neck and hid it beneath her clothes.

"I'll go into the Big Top," M.R. told Sarah when Linette left. "I want to make sure we have good seats."

He turned to Kate, and she knew that if her braid were down, he would have yanked it. "This time I'm going to watch you every minute."

––––––––––

Before long, Roberto returned, still wearing his polka-dot costume. In spite of the hot day, his whiteface makeup looked neat, his large smiling mouth and great black eyebrows perfectly in place.

Sarah stood up. "Linette asked me to give you this," she said as she handed Roberto the small cloth bag.

When he nodded his thanks, Sarah turned to Kate, "I'll see you after the show." She hurried away to join M.R.

Roberto slipped his hand into a pocket. He moved quickly, as if eager to change into the suit for his riding act. When he started toward the dressing tent, Mitsy barked at him.

Instead of going into the tent, the clown walked away. When he reached the door to the animal cages, he glanced back.

As he vanished from sight, Kate remembered Roberto's words, "Dogs know human nature." She started after the clown.

Just then Anders came around the dressing tent, once again wearing his stilts.

"C'mon!" Kate told him. Still holding Mitsy's leash, Kate ran toward the door out of the backyard.

"What's wrong?" Anders asked as he followed.

"Mitsy barked at the clown," Kate said.

"Oh-oh!" Her brother didn't slow down. "Then it's not Roberto. It must be Leo!"

In great long strides, Anders passed Kate. At the opening in the tent wall, he bent down to get through. When they reached the other side of the cages, Kate was close behind.

Together they hurried down the walkway, past the entrance to the sideshow.

"There he is!" Kate exclaimed as she spied the polka-dot costume ahead of them. In spite of his floppy shoes, the clown moved quickly.

When he left the walkway, Anders followed. His long legs reached out, sure and steady. In spite of the extra padding Kate wore, she managed to keep up.

Near the lemonade tent, the clown looked back, then picked up his speed. Walking faster, he disappeared into the crowd.

"Where is he?" Kate asked.

Her brother kept on. "I'm tall enough to see him." Anders slipped around a cluster of people. Beyond the food tents lay a farmhouse. When the crowd thinned out, Kate saw the polka dots again.

The clown was running straight toward a barn with a huge circus poster covering its side. A ladder still leaned against the wall.

"We've got him now," Anders muttered, and walked even faster.

Kate saw what he meant. A high board fence blocked the clown's way.

Near the barn, the clown stopped, as if wondering where to go. As he looked around, Kate and Anders hurried over the uneven ground.

Suddenly Mitsy jerked hard. Caught by surprise, Kate lost hold of the leash. The little dog ran straight toward the clown. A few feet away from him, Mitsy planted her feet and barked.

The clown raised his hand as though he would strike her.

Mitsy leaped away and barked again.

Once more the clown threatened her. Mitsy fled to the ladder leaning against the wall. Scampering up, she balanced near the top, out of harm's way.

"Stop!" Anders cried to the clown. "We want to talk to you."

As the man turned toward Anders, Mitsy leaped on the clown's back. Caught by surprise, the clown tumbled to the ground. He and the dog rolled in the dirt.

Anders had almost reached the clown when he stepped into a hole. Frantically he waved his arms, trying to keep his balance.

Instead, he rocked one way, then the other. At the last moment he crouched low and crashed forward on his hands and knees.

Kate forgot about the clown and ran to Anders. He lay sprawled in the dirt, moaning.

"Are you all right?" Kate asked.

Anders moaned again. Falling from such a great height had hurt, Kate could tell. Yet her brother struggled to sit up.

"Roberto had me wear extra padding," he said. "Just in case."

Kate whirled around, remembering the clown. He had seen his opportunity. Once again he had run away. This time he was gone.

As though every movement hurt, Anders rolled over. "I can't believe I did that!"

"I can. The ground is really uneven."

Anders struggled to his knees, then realized he couldn't stand up without help. Quickly he rolled up the legs of his long trousers, then crawled over to a nearby hay wagon. There he pulled himself up.

Mitsy came to Kate willingly and looked none the worse for her battle. Together they all started back to the Big Top.

Anders still looked upset. "It's my fault that guy got away!"

Kate shook her head. "No, it's not. You can't help that there's a hole in the ground."

"Same height, same weight," Anders grumbled as they hurried along.

Kate knew he was talking about the clown. "But all at once Mitsy didn't like him. Can we trust her judgment?"

"I think so. We'll know when we get back."

"Anders, Sarah gave the clown a little cloth bag from Linette." Kate felt deeply troubled by the whole thing. "Linette asked her to keep it safe. What do you suppose is in it?"

Anders shook his head.

"Remember when I thought Linette slipped something to Roberto? During her act she can't have something dangling around her neck. Whatever is in the bag, it must be valuable."

"And you think Roberto locks it in his trunk before his act?"

"Roberto could lose it during that horse act," Kate said.

By now they had reached the walkway, but Kate was running out of breath. "Slow down just a bit, will you?" she asked. "I can't keep up to you."

"Yah, sure, little sister." In spite of all that had happened, Anders grinned.

Kate was still thinking. "Wouldn't it be easier just to keep something valuable in the trunk? Instead of passing a small bag back and forth?"

Anders shook his head. "Not the way those trunks get tossed around. Off a train, on a train, every twenty-four hours. Circus people really know how to do things. But I wonder if anything ever gets lost or dropped or damaged in some way?"

When Kate and Anders reached the backyard, they found Roberto there. "Better hurry," he said. "There are only two more songs before the walk-around."

Roberto was dressed in the yellow and black suit for his riding act. Seeing him, Kate had her answer.

The clown could not possibly have gotten away from them, removed his makeup, and changed clothes in such a short time. On such a hot day, he'd be warm and sweaty from running back.

Quickly Kate and Anders told Roberto everything that had happened. "Mitsy barked at the clown," Kate finished. "That's how I guessed it wasn't you."

Roberto moaned. "It's gone?" he asked. "The little bag Linette gave Sarah is really gone?"

"What's in it?" Kate wanted to know.

But Roberto moaned again. His face was gray-white as he warned, "If you see Linette, don't tell her what happened. I'll talk to her after her act."

As Kate and Anders started for the Big Top, Roberto went to find a policeman.

————

During the evening performance, Kate learned what it meant when people said the show must go on. All around her were circus workers and performers who knew everything that had happened that day. More than once, Kate saw a nervous hand, a worried look. Each person seemed to have one question: *What will happen next?*

Yet all of them did their best to pretend nothing was wrong. They played to the audience, and the crowd loved it.

Near the end of the show, Kate again stood near the back door where she could watch the aerialists.

Once Linette's hand reached out and grabbed only space. Just in time a trapeze swung back into her grasp. Was it part of the act, to worry the crowd? Or had it been a near miss? Kate wasn't sure.

When it happened again, Kate had her answer. Then, as Linette flew toward Will, she almost crashed into his head. Only his quick movement avoided a collision.

Near the end of the act, Linette's hands came within a hairsbreadth of missing Will's catch. When the crowd gasped, Kate glanced toward Roberto. By now he was wearing clown makeup that covered his worry. But his body looked tense.

When the act was over, Kate breathed a sigh of relief. She and Anders joined in the final walk-around, heard the ringmaster's last words: "May all your days be circus days!"

As they followed Roberto into the backyard, Kate felt as if she couldn't believe her eyes. Already the cookhouse tent was down, and the cages filled with animals were gone. The horse top had also vanished. The lot seemed strangely empty.

Roberto pulled Linette to one side and told her what had happened. Even in the dim light, the pretty aerialist looked white.

"Sarah gave Leo the diamonds?" she asked. "She *gave* them to him?"

Roberto nodded. "He was wearing my extra clown costume."

"Diamonds?" Kate asked. So that's what was in the little cloth bag.

"Diamonds!" Linette exclaimed. "And now, they're stolen!"

16

Roberto's Warning

Circus people move around so much," Roberto explained. "When we earn money, it's hard to buy a house or other property. For years I've invested in diamonds."

"And now Leo has them." Kate felt sick.

Roberto nodded, his face grim. "Everything I've saved, my entire life." Sadness clung to him like an old coat.

Linette shook her head. Her eyes sparkled with anger. "That terrible, terrible man! It's everything we have!"

"No, that's not so." Roberto took Linette's hand. "We still have each other."

Linette nodded, as though unable to speak.

"I'm going to miss you," Kate said as she and Linette changed clothes in the women's side of the dressing tent. "I've known you just a few hours, but I'll miss you."

"I'll miss you, too, Kate," Linette said softly. "I wish you could have been here on a good day. Usually everything goes well."

By the time they finished changing, men were waiting to take down the dressing tent. Already Roberto was ready to drive away a wagon loaded with equipment.

"We'll come to the train," Kate said quickly when Linette would have said goodbye. *Somehow, somewhere, we'll find Leo before you leave!* Kate wanted to tell her.

She and Anders found M.R. and Sarah waiting for them. When Sarah heard about the diamonds, she couldn't believe what she had done. *"I gave diamonds away?"*

Tears filled her eyes. "That's what Linette asked me to keep safe? How could I do such a dumb thing?"

"It wasn't your fault," Kate said quickly. "You don't see Roberto very often, and the clown's makeup covered his face."

Just the same, a lump filled Kate's throat. Together the four walked back into the Big Top.

The three large rings stood empty, silent. A man from the work crew swept the red carpet. Other workers took down the rigging from which Linette had flown as gracefully as a bird.

When everything was out of the tent, a man warned them that they must leave. "Big Top coming down!" he shouted. "Big Top coming down!"

From a safe distance Kate and the others watched. Like a giant balloon losing its air, the Big Top sank to the ground. Kate felt sad that the circus day was already over.

"It's all done," she said dully.

M.R. grinned. "Guess so."

Men rolled up the tent and loaded canvas and poles onto wagons. Still other workers walked across the lot, searching for anything that might have been left. Somehow the tent city seemed like a dream.

A whistle blew. As horses and wagons moved out, Kate ached for what was gone. Worst of all, they hadn't solved the mystery surrounding Roberto and Linette.

With all her heart Kate had wanted to find Leo. Instead, the man seemed to have gotten away. The circus was leaving.

Kate turned to Anders. He was looking around, as if he, too, hated to see the tent city vanish.

"I wonder if I'll ever be a stilt clown again," he said.

"You were a good one," Sarah said. She was still trying to blink away her tears. "Maybe you'll have another chance."

"What shall we do?" Kate asked the other three.

Anders shrugged. "Might as well go to the train."

Kate sighed. "We're running out of time. Leo will get away." She hated even the thought of that escape.

"Well, you know what Granny would say." Anders sounded as if he were trying to cheer Sarah up. " 'If at first you don't succeed, try, try again.' "

When Sarah laughed through her tears, Kate felt better. Even so, she couldn't shake off her disappointment. What would happen to Roberto and Linette? When would Leo strike again?

Kate and Anders, Sarah and M.R. followed the flickering flame of smudge pots to the train. Horses were pulling circus wagons up the runs and across the flatcars to the right place. Once more, the beautiful wagons with gold leaf were covered by canvas.

Linette and Roberto waited near a passenger car, ready to board.

"Say hi to Granny for me," Roberto told Sarah. "Tell her I wish I could have gotten away to see her."

"We're sorry," Kate said quietly when she said goodbye. "We wanted to help you, but we didn't."

"Yes, you did," Linette answered. "You did everything you could. And as Roberto said, we still have each other." She looked up to meet Roberto's gaze. The clown smiled down at her.

Then Roberto turned to Anders. "When do you leave town?"

"Monday morning. There isn't a train to Frederic till then."

"We told the police about the diamonds and everything else. They'll be watching the trains."

Roberto lowered his voice. "Leo won't dare catch a ride on ours, not even in disguise. All the circus people will watch for anyone they don't know. But Leo will try to slip out of town as soon as he can."

"We'll watch the trains too," Anders promised. "I hope we find Leo before he finds you."

Roberto nodded, as though he dreaded having Leo follow him. Yet he had his own warning. "If you find out even one thing, talk to the police. Leo knows you want to stop what he's

doing. Just when you think everything's all right, he'll strike
again."

In spite of Linette's warm farewell hug, Kate trembled.

———————

In the clear, moonlit night Kate and Anders, Sarah and M.R.
waited until the train chugged out of town.

During the day Kate had barely had time to talk to M.R. It
was late now—very late. Yet all of tomorrow stretched ahead of
them. Not until evening would M.R. and Sarah take the train
back to Minneapolis. Before then, Kate would make every moment count.

As the last car disappeared down the track, she and M.R.
started back to Granny's.

"Mama said to tell you that church will be at eleven o'clock
tomorrow," Kate said.

"Church?" M.R. asked. "You go to church even when you're
away from home?"

Kate stepped back in surprise. "Why, yes." She had taken it
for granted that they'd all go to church on Sunday morning.

"Do your folks make you go?"

"They *expect* me to go," Kate said with dignity. "But I also
want to go."

"That's the strangest thing I ever heard! Why do you want to
do that?"

Suddenly Kate remembered she wasn't going to talk with
M.R. about God.

"Why do you want to go to church?" he asked again.

Inwardly Kate groaned. Like Sarah, M.R. was asking questions Kate didn't want to answer. Now M.R. waited.

Kate swallowed hard, fighting against what she needed to
say. No matter how much she wanted to lie, Kate knew she
couldn't. "Because church means a lot to me," she finally answered.

"It does?"

Just then Sarah and Anders caught up with them. M.R. made
a face, as though Kate was the strangest person he'd ever met.

"Kate says she wants to go to church tomorrow."

Sarah did not laugh. Instead, she watched Kate, as if to hear what she'd say.

Kate's stomach knotted. So Sarah also thought she was strange. Kate wanted to run away from both of them.

But Sarah touched Kate's arm. "Why does it mean something to you?"

This time Kate understood the difference between Sarah and M.R. Sarah really wanted to know.

How can I possibly explain? Kate wondered. Even the idea frightened her.

She glanced toward Anders. He grinned, as though saying, "I'm with you, but you tell 'em."

Then for Kate the words came. "If something happened to me . . ." Kate paused.

M.R. jumped in. "Aw, Kate, what's going to happen to you?"

Suddenly Kate remembered the mother lion. As though it were happening again, she saw the lion coming toward her.

Just thinking about it, Kate grew tense. "Well, I suppose I could have gotten chewed up by the lion."

The grin left M.R.'s face. For an instant he looked embarrassed.

In the quiet, Kate spoke again. "If something happened to me, I would go to heaven. But Jesus also helps me now—every day. With everything I face."

"Kate," M.R. said, and the tone of his voice had changed. "If it helps you to believe that, it's all right. Girls need religion more than boys."

Anders stiffened. Kate guessed what he was about to say. Anders believed all the same things she did. Yet before he could speak, M.R. cut him off. "You know, Kate, we don't have to waste time talking about something like church."

"I'm not so sure about that," Sarah answered. Her beautiful brown eyes looked thoughtful.

———

"Kate?" Sarah asked softly as the two of them entered the bedroom they shared with Tina.

The room was still warm from the heat of the day, but Tina was sound asleep. Kate and Sarah sat down on the floor near the open windows to talk without waking the little girl.

Moonlight fell across Sarah's face. "Kate, you said that God helps you when you're scared. But what did you say would happen to you if that lion—" Sarah stopped, as though afraid to say the words.

"If the lion hurt me?"

"Even *killed* you?" Sarah's question was little more than a whisper.

"I would go to heaven."

"How do you know—*really* know?" Sarah's pretty eyes were troubled.

Kate drew a deep breath. It seemed so strange. In all the years she and Sarah were friends, they had never talked about what they believed.

Quietly Kate began to tell Sarah what she knew about God's love. How He sent His Son into the world as a baby. Then how Jesus died on the cross.

"He was perfect," Kate explained. "Jesus never did anything wrong. But He let himself be killed."

"Why?" Sarah sounded as if she were testing every one of Kate's words.

"So we can ask forgiveness for the wrong things we do. When we tell Jesus we're sorry, He forgives us."

"And He helps you every day? Now, I mean?" Large tears stood in Sarah's eyes. "With everything that makes you scared?"

Kate nodded.

"I want that," Sarah said. "Tell me how."

"You tell Jesus that you're sorry," Kate answered. "Sorry for everything wrong you've done. You ask Him to forgive you. To come into your life."

When Sarah finished praying, Kate reached out and hugged her.

———

Long after Sarah fell asleep, Kate lay awake in the bed the

two of them shared. In the darkness Kate stared up at the ceiling.

One moment she felt happy, thinking about Sarah's prayer. But then, as the sun edged up over the horizon, Kate remembered Roberto and Linette.

The pain in Roberto's eyes would be hard to forget. All the money he had saved, all the years he had worked were lost in one moment of theft.

Trying not to wake Sarah, Kate slipped from bed. Sitting on the floor next to the window, she looked down on the street that passed the house.

In the last few days Kate had seen a terrible kind of getting even. Over and over Leo had tried to hurt Roberto because the aerialist had taken a stand for what he believed.

In his fight against Leo's stealing, Roberto had been physically hurt. But now, Kate knew there was something even more important. *Roberto's spirit is still strong. He'll keep on standing up for what he knows is right.*

As the first cool breeze touched Kate's face, she caught a shadow down the street. A dark shape moved closer.

Kate leaned forward to see. The man who walked below stayed on the grass instead of on the dirt street.

Why? Kate wondered. *Because the grass muffles the sound of his steps?*

He seemed a stranger, but Roberto said Leo was a master of disguises. *What if I look right at him and don't recognize him?*

As the man passed the house, he continued west toward the edge of town. Kate's gaze followed him. She could not push aside her questions. *Could that possibly be Leo?*

17

Special Friend

A few hours later, Kate woke up feeling excited. M.R. and Sarah would leave on the evening train to Minneapolis. Yet they would have the whole day together.

Then Kate remembered Leo. *What will he try next? What if he's watching me, and I don't even know it?*

As Kate bounded out of bed, she tried to push her worries aside. Sarah looked happy today, more peaceful. Every time Kate thought about the reason why, she felt good.

Kate put on her prettiest dress, the white one she wore only on Sundays and important occasions.

When they came home from church, Kate helped Mama pack a big picnic lunch.

Granny was feeling stronger now, strong enough for Sarah to go home to Minneapolis. But when the family asked Granny to join their picnic, she waved her hand at such a silly idea. "Oh, no, no. You go along now. Have a good time!"

Mama had also invited Darren. Together all of them set out for the city park—the Glen, as Darren called it. Papa and Anders each carried a basket. Mama walked with baby Bernie in her arms.

Before long, Papa passed his basket to M.R. and took the baby from Mama. At two and a half months, Bernie was getting heavy to carry.

Darren knew every inch of River Falls. Still barefooted, he led them past the homes on the west side of the river. Tina skipped along beside him and Lars. Anders and Sarah kept up the pace, while M.R. and Kate followed behind.

As much as Kate wanted to forget Leo, she soon found it impossible. Everywhere she looked, Kate wondered if she was seeing him. More than once, she compared a man's size and weight to what she remembered about Leo.

Yet something else bothered Kate still more. Today she was going to make sure there was no argument with M.R. With her whole heart she wanted to please him. *I'll do everything right so he likes me more than all those Minneapolis girls!*

In the midday sunlight M.R. looked even more handsome than yesterday. Now he pushed aside the hair falling over his forehead. "I want to talk to you," he said.

Kate's heart leaped. *What does he want to tell me?*

Before M.R. could utter another word, Tina joined them. "Darren said there's a waterfall in the park."

M.R. groaned, and Tina looked at him. "Is there something wrong with you?"

Tina slipped her hand into Kate's. "We get to walk close to the waterfall, Darren says."

The little girl was still with them when they left Falls Street behind. Her white-blond hair curled around the edge of her warm face.

She looked up at Kate. "You took good care of me yesterday. That lion really scared me."

"Me too," Kate said softly. "I'm awfully glad you're all right." Though Kate wanted to talk to M.R., Tina meant especially much to her today.

Soon they crossed a railroad track, then the bridge over the main channel of the Kinnickinnic River. Tina kept talking.

By the time they reached Cascade Street, M.R. looked impatient. Kate wondered if she should ask Tina to leave. Yet Kate knew that soon the little girl would go on to someone else.

Each time M.R. said something, he talked only to Kate. Whenever Tina could get in a word, she chattered on as though she didn't notice.

"Tina!" M.R. said finally. He sounded angry. "Why don't you walk with Lars and Darren?"

A hurt look flashed through Tina's blue eyes. "Because Kate's my sister!" she said.

"Kate swallowed hard, feeling torn between the two of them. Then she squeezed Tina's hand. "It's all right," Kate told her. "I love you."

"I love you too." Tina squeezed back. Without another word she left them.

"You hurt Tina!" Kate told M.R. In spite of her plans to please him, the words slipped out.

"I want to talk to *you*," M.R. answered. His smile flashed. "We have only a few more hours together."

Immediately Kate felt ashamed. "You're right," she said quickly. Yet swifter than an arrow, a memory pierced her mind— the way M.R. treated Darren the day before. *Erik would have been nice to Tina.*

The next moment Kate pushed the thought away. *Erik knows her. It's different for M.R.*

At the same time, Kate felt uncomfortable. *What's wrong with me, always comparing the two boys?*

Near the Cascade Mill a flight of steps led down the steep banks to the South Fork. In the already hot day, Kate welcomed the shade of tall trees.

On one of the landings she and M.R. stopped. M.R. yanked her braid in their special signal. In spite of her mixed-up feelings, Kate smiled.

From here she could see upstream to where the water swirled between steep limestone walls. Close by, the river plunged over a dam, creating a waterfall.

At the bottom of the steps, a bridge led across to the opposite bank. Kate stopped on the bridge and felt mist rising from the waterfall. The coolness felt good on her face.

Downstream, paths led the length of the Glen—the quiet, narrow valley between steep banks. *What a romantic spot!* Kate thought. *The perfect place for what M.R. wants to tell me!*

She and M.R., Anders and Sarah left the others to follow one of the paths along the South Fork. Near the path, the river tumbled around large rocks.

Soon they reached the place where the South Fork joined the main channel. On a high bluff across the river stood the city's power plant. Nearby was the dam used to make electricity.

As they came out from the shady Glen, the sun felt even hotter than yesterday. On the treeless riverbank, the air seemed to hover above them, weighing down everything it touched.

Sarah and Anders soon started back to the Glen. As Kate followed them, M.R. began to drop back.

"How can I talk to you when you always have a brother or sister around?"

"Well, you can talk now," Kate said calmly. But her heart raced. *He wants to tell me something really special!*

"You're different than you used to be," M.R. said.

Anders heard him. Glancing back, he winked.

Kate felt a flush of embarrassment rush to her face. She slowed down to put more distance between Anders and M.R. "Different?" she asked.

Erik had told her that she was different from other girls. Often Kate clutched that memory to herself. Was M.R. saying the same thing?

"What do you mean—different?" Kate asked.

"You're not as much of a scaredy-cat."

If only you knew, Kate thought. *Right now I'm scared about what you're going to say.*

"You've gotten prettier," M.R. said softly.

Kate smiled. It was just what she had hoped—that she would look beautiful to him.

"You surprised me," he went on. "I didn't expect you to grow up to be so pretty."

For some reason, a flash of anger swept through Kate. "And what if I hadn't?"

"If you hadn't what?" Clearly M.R. didn't understand what she was asking.

"If I hadn't grown up to be pretty?" Kate's voice had the feel of steel running through it. "Would you still want me to be your friend?"

M.R. stared at her, as though debating his answer. Finally he shrugged. "Well, it didn't happen, so what difference does it make?"

Kate sighed. "A lot of difference." Yes, she wanted to be pretty. Even yesterday it was all that seemed to matter. But something had changed in twenty-four hours. Now she wanted more.

"Aren't there any other reasons for liking me?" Kate asked as they followed the path back to the bridge. Suddenly she realized she'd forgotten all about pleasing M.R. Deep inside, she felt a small ache.

M.R. circled a rock. "Sure," he said, as though not quite certain how to answer. A grin spread across his good-looking face.

But it did not warm Kate. Her heart felt closed in by ice. "Don't you care about what I *am*?"

M.R. looked puzzled. "What you *are*?"

"What I *am*." Because of her talk with Sarah, Kate felt more hopeful that M.R. would understand. "The way I think. What I believe."

"What you believe?" His voice sounded sharp. "Aw, Kate, don't start that stuff again."

Inside Kate, the ache was growing. *This romantic place,* she told herself. *But there's nothing here.*

When she and M.R. reached the bridge again, they followed Anders and Sarah up the steps on the other side of the river. At the top of the hill, the land leveled out beneath tall oaks.

An American flag flew from a pole on the roof of a log shelter. Inside the building was a small cookstove and silverware and dishes for people to use.

Near the shelter, Lars was pumping water into a pail. Soon Mama had coffee boiling over an open fire. She laid out a feast that included good bread from home and baked chicken from Granny's.

Kate sat down at the picnic table. *Maybe I misunderstood what M.R. meant*, she thought, still wanting to hope.

Yet a question kept nudging at her mind. *Does M.R. choose his friends to make himself look more popular?* Kate couldn't help but think of the ways Erik had helped her with what she believed.

As Sarah joined her at the table, Kate tried to push the questions aside. But when she looked around, she remembered Leo. In the large park there were a million places where he could hide.

"Sarah, what's on the west side of town?" Kate asked. "Are there any empty buildings?"

Sarah thought for a moment. "On the very edge of River Falls, just beyond the houses, there's a starch factory. After harvest, farmers bring in their potatoes."

"But no one is there now?"

Sarah shook her head. "Not even a watchman. Why do you ask?"

"If Leo's still in town, he needs a place to hide." Kate remembered the man on the street, walking west.

Sarah looked worried. "Kate, if you go there, you make sure you take a policeman along. Promise?"

"Promise."

"Leo's a dangerous man."

He'll show up when you least expect him, Roberto had said. Kate wished she could forget about Leo. He seemed like a dark cloud on a day that should be sunny.

As soon as they finished eating, Anders jumped up. "Let's go for a walk."

When he stretched out a hand and helped Sarah to her feet, Kate wanted to giggle. Never before had she seen her brother so helpful to anyone. Sarah and M.R. seemed glad to follow.

Instead of returning to the Glen, Anders started across the flat area on which they had picnicked. On this hot afternoon the oaks offered welcome shade.

When they came to the edge of the steep hill, they found that trees blocked a view of the river below. Anders followed the rim of the hill until he came to an opening.

Off in the distance, the main channel of the river wound around the flat ground of the river bottom. At least three peninsulas of long grass reached out into the waterway.

Farther on, Anders found a path and started downward. Sarah followed, then Kate and M.R. Now and then Kate had to catch a branch to keep from tumbling ahead on the steep ground.

At the bottom, tall marsh grass grew in the lowlands close to the river. The three- or four-foot grass hung over narrow trails made by animals going to the river to drink.

Soon Kate found a wider path and started toward the water. After a short distance, she heard a sharp cry. With whirring wings, a bird flew up, directly in front of her.

Her heart pounding, Kate leaped back. The bird landed about twenty feet away. Where the path widened, Kate could see its drab-colored feathers.

With both wings hanging down, the bird ran along the ground. "Oh, she's hurt," Kate said.

"She wants to be seen," Anders told her. "It's a partridge."

He stepped into the long grass at the side of the trail. Again the hen flew up, its wings beating violently.

When Anders backed out of the grass, he held a chick in his cupped hands.

"The hen?" Kate asked. "She was trying to draw us away?"

Anders nodded. "To give her chicks a chance to escape. A partridge doesn't put on as good a show as a killdeer, but it's the same trick."

Carefully he held out the chick for the others to see. The dull, soft feathers covered even its legs. "Must be a late brood."

"What do you mean?" Sarah asked.

"Usually a grouse lays its eggs in May. They hatch a few weeks later. If the first nest is destroyed, she'll lay more eggs."

"Is the nest here?"

Anders tipped his head toward the woods. "Somewhere in

there, I think. The hen probably led them here to pick insects off the grass."

Gently Anders set the chick down in the center of the trail. For an instant it stood there, then disappeared. Kate heard the sound of peeping from the long grass.

"Will it be all right?" Sarah still sounded concerned.

Anders nodded. "The mother will find it."

Setting off again, Anders led them down the peninsula toward the river. In the heat of the afternoon Kate pushed back her bangs and remembered her white dress. Carefully she held it away from the long grass.

M.R. dragged behind. Before long, Kate realized he was dropping back on purpose.

"When you go home, will you write to me?" he asked to Kate's surprise. "I want to see you again—to be special friends."

Kate stared at him. For as long as she could remember, M.R. had been part of her dreams. Once there was nothing she would have liked better. But now—

The ache was still there, deep inside, as if her heart had been squeezed.

"I'm sorry," Kate said softly. "It's fun to be with you. I like you, but—"

"But what?"

"We don't think the same things are important."

"What do you mean?" M.R. asked.

Kate took a deep breath. She didn't know when she had decided what to say, but all at once the words were there. "God really means a lot to me—especially after yesterday."

This time it was M.R.'s turn to stare. "Are you serious? You don't want to be special friends because of what you believe about God?"

Kate felt as if her face were burning with embarrassment. *I've always liked M.R.,* she thought. For an instant doubt flashed through her mind. *Is what I believe worth fighting for?*

As though sensing her doubt, M.R. grinned. "I'll talk you out of that foolish idea."

Kate straightened, flipped her braid over her shoulder. "No, you won't."

"Yes, I will." He sounded so sure of himself that it frightened Kate.

Maybe you would at that, Kate thought. The idea scared her. If she spent much time with M.R., he could swing her around to whatever he thought. *Do I want to give up what I believe in order to be his special friend?*

Kate turned away. As she started back over the trail, there was something she knew with certainty. *The more I see him, the more I'll like him. It would be even harder to say goodbye.*

When M.R. hurried after her, Kate quickened her steps. She wanted to get away before M.R. convinced her that he was more important than her beliefs.

"Hey, where's the fire?" he called.

But Kate walked even faster. Not for anything in the world would she let him know how much she wanted to be his special friend.

18

Trouble Ahead!

*W*hen it was time for the evening train, the family and Darren walked with Sarah and M.R. to the depot.

"We need to watch every person who gets on the train," Anders reminded Kate in a low voice. "If Leo tries to leave town, we have to help the police catch him."

"Won't they be watching?" she asked. She still ached from her talk with M.R. She found it hard even to think about Leo.

"Roberto talked to them," Anders said. "But we've seen Leo. They haven't."

As the train rumbled into the station, Kate glanced around. A policeman stood near the depot, his face alert. Another man pushed a large cart filled with suitcases, but he, too, seemed to be studying every face.

As the trainmen loaded the baggage car, Darren looked up at Kate. "You go home tomorrow morning?"

Kate nodded. "Early."

The boy turned to Lars. "I have to go now," he said. "I promised Mum I'd be home before dark."

Lars looked lost, and Kate understood the feeling. In these two days the two boys had become good friends. Neither wanted to say goodbye.

"I'll see you," Darren said bravely. He looked at Lars, then at Kate.

Suddenly Lars sat down on the ground. He pulled off his shoes, then glanced toward Mama. When she nodded her permission, Lars handed the shoes to Darren. "For you," Lars said.

"For *me*?"

"Anders has a pair at home I can wear. His feet are too big for them."

"You're sure I can have them?" Darren asked.

"Sure!"

Darren clutched the shoes to his chest. "Thank you! I'll wear 'em to school when it starts."

For a moment he stood there, meeting Lars's gaze, as though wondering what more to say. "I wish you lived in River Falls," he blurted out finally.

Once again he looked at Kate, then Lars. "See you!" Darren whirled around, as though trying to hide how he felt. Then he was gone.

Sarah and Anders were still talking when the conductor called, "All ah-boarrrrd!"

Sarah hurried over to Kate. A smile curved her pretty lips. "I'll never forget our time together," she said. "I'll always remember the meaning of my prayer."

"So will I," Kate answered. "You're the best friend I could ever have!" Kate opened her arms, and they hugged each other.

It was even more difficult saying goodbye to M.R. "I wish things had been different," she told him.

"I'll see you again," he answered.

Kate shook her head. "I don't think so." Even in this moment she wanted to be honest. "Not when we disagree on what's most important."

M.R. grinned, as though unwilling to accept defeat. "I won't forget you, Kate. You'll see that God isn't worth bothering your head about."

The confidence in his voice scared Kate. She tried to smile as though she thought he was joking. Yet she knew that he wasn't.

M.R. was the last to climb onto the train. At the top of the steps he turned toward Kate and waved.

When he and Sarah disappeared through the door, Mama and Papa started back to Granny's. Kate stayed on the platform, as though unable to move.

Before long, she saw Sarah waving to her from one of the windows. Kate smiled and blew her friend a kiss.

Then M.R. was there, framed in the square of glass. Kate waved back and tried to smile.

Moments later, the train blew a warning whistle. Steam hissed, wheels turned. The train chugged out of the station.

"I hope I see Sarah soon," Anders said.

When Kate didn't answer, he looked into her face. "Not the way you thought it'd be, huh?"

Kate felt embarrassed by how much Anders noticed, how much he knew about her. She dreaded his teasing.

But her brother surprised her. "It'll turn out all right," he said gruffly.

Kate doubted it. As the caboose disappeared, tears filled her eyes. She blinked, tried to brush them away. Instead, they streamed down her cheeks.

———

As Kate started away from the platform, she dragged her feet. The July afternoon seemed even hotter. Again she pushed back her bangs. Her long braid felt hot on her back.

"Well, our friend Leo didn't climb onto the train," Anders said.

"You're sure?"

"I checked every passenger that climbed aboard. The height, the weight, the build. Even if Leo wore padding or dressed to look like a woman, there was nothing that matched."

Kate sighed. The air was so heavy she felt as if she couldn't breathe.

Yet it was more than the weather. Seldom had Kate felt so discouraged. All her dreams about seeing M.R.—destroyed! Nothing had turned out the way she hoped.

And Roberto and Linette! People they liked and really wanted to help. How could everything go so wrong?

Then Kate remembered Sarah. Sarah wanting to know more. Sarah wondering what had given Kate courage. Sarah praying.

Kate straightened her shoulders. As she turned to see if Lars and Tina were following, Kate glanced down. On the ground close to the end wall of the depot, she saw peanut shells. Something clicked in her mind.

Leo. The snubber. The man near the lion cage. They all ate peanuts. Even the man she had seen the first night in River Falls had bulging pockets.

"Well, well, well," Anders said when Kate told him what she was thinking.

"It looks as if Leo stood here watching," Kate said. "He must have seen us and decided not to take the train."

The idea made her uncomfortable. At the same time she had new hope.

When they looked for the policeman, he had already gone. Quickly Kate repeated what Sarah said about the starch factory.

"Leo could be staying there. Or maybe he's left a trail of peanut shells. If we find that he has, we can get the police."

Anders explained the reason for their search to Lars and Tina, then said, "Let's spread out. Maybe we'll see something more."

Tina was the one who discovered cast-off shells near the tracks going south to Ellsworth. Along Pine Street, Lars found more. For the next half block there was nothing.

Again the four spread out. As Kate searched, she noticed the strange color of the sky. It was too early to be dark, but they seemed to be losing the light.

"Anders," Kate said quietly. She didn't want to frighten Tina, but she felt uneasy. "What should we do?"

Anders, too, was looking at the sky. Not a leaf stirred on the trees. "Get back to Granny's," he said.

"But Leo?"

"We shouldn't stay out in bad weather. It's too dangerous."

"Let's look a little longer," Kate begged.

"Only a few more minutes," he said. "Whatever is coming is moving in fast."

Ahead of them, the railroad tracks crossed the street. On the other side, Kate spotted more peanut shells. Then a cast-off shell led them onto the Maple Street bridge. Leo's trail was leading them toward Main Street. Yet time was running out.

From the bridge Kate looked southwest toward a mill. Through an opening between the trees, she saw the sky. It was dark, almost black, yet green at the same time.

Again Kate felt the need to hurry. With all her heart she wanted to keep on searching. Yet she and Anders were responsible for the others.

"Let's race," Kate said to Tina, and the little girl ran ahead.

Just then a horse and buggy turned onto the bridge. Catching up, Kate grabbed Tina's hand.

When the buggy passed, Tina darted away again. Glancing back, she grinned at Kate. A moment later, Tina ran headlong into a man's stomach.

"Oooof!" he exclaimed, and Kate almost laughed aloud.

But the man pulled down his hat. Stepping aside, he circled Tina. With a quick glance toward Kate, he kept on toward the west side of the bridge.

Who is he? Kate thought. She had barely seen the man's eyes. Yet without glasses they seemed familiar.

Kate whirled around. Instead of a battered hat, the man wore a new one. Instead of work clothes, a nice suit. While Kate stared, the man turned.

Clean-shaven instead of a stubby beard. Light brown hair.

Then the man's gaze met Kate's. As if held by a magnet, she stood there, unable to move.

In another instant the man turned away. In the greenish light Kate saw what she had missed before. Below his hat, the man's hair came to a stiff, square point, just above his collar.

Leo!

Kate's stomach tightened. "Anders," she said quickly. "Lars! It's Leo! He must have started toward Main Street, then changed his mind."

Just then Leo took a quick left.

"He's going toward that mill," Anders said. "Let's follow him."

They hurried back over the bridge in the direction from which they'd come. As they reached the west side once more, Leo disappeared behind some trees.

Anders started to run toward a large building with a sign saying *Greenwood Mill*. At the far end, he stopped and waited for the rest of them to catch up. "Shhhh!" he warned.

Anders looked around the corner of the building. "He's slowing down. Probably thinks he's left us behind."

As Kate edged out, Leo glanced back. Kate ducked behind the corner, but it was too late.

"He saw me."

Anders groaned. "Aw, Kate. Your curiosity always gets us into trouble."

Carefully he looked around the corner. "Leo knows we can identify him. He's running again."

Anders turned to Lars. "Go get Papa. Tell him to bring the police."

"Take Tina to Mama," Kate said.

But Anders shook his head. "He'll go faster alone."

"Tell Papa that Leo's going toward Glen Park," Anders said. "We'll follow as long as it's safe."

Like a scared rabbit, Lars raced off on bare feet. As he disappeared, thunder rumbled in the distance.

Anders motioned for Kate and Tina to follow. On the other side of the mill the railroad tracks made a Y. One set of tracks went left over a bridge crossing the river. Leo ran along the other tracks, staying to the right.

In the greenish dusk, Anders dodged between trees. Kate clung to Tina's hand, pulling her along.

Once Anders stopped, as though to find direction. Again Kate noticed the stillness. Even the birds were strangely silent. Then Leo stepped out from behind a tree.

A spatter of rain struck Kate's face, then dried up as they ran on. Through the pounding of her heart, Kate felt the quiet. The heat. The strange half-light.

Ahead of them, the land dropped away steeply to the river. One tall chimney pointed to the sky. Beyond was the electric plant Kate had seen from Glen Park.

She and Anders crossed the bridge near the light plant, still running. As they started across a pasture, Tina's breath came in great long gasps. The little girl had done her best to keep up. Yet far ahead, the man was slipping away.

Then lightning flashed across the sky. Like a kettle drum, thunder rumbled. The green sky grew darker by the moment.

Lightning streaked from cloud to ground. As Tina shrank back, all thought of Leo vanished from Kate's mind.

Frantically Kate glanced around. "Where can we go?" she called to Anders. He, too, was looking for shelter.

Then in the middle of the pasture Kate spied a tall oak. With its trunk at least three feet across, it stretched upward, possibly a hundred feet. Like long arms, its spreading branches reached out.

"Let's get under that tree," Kate shouted above the thunder. Her brother shook his head.

"C'mon!" Kate started toward the tree.

"No!" Anders cried. Breaking his headlong pace, he stood still. "It's the only tree around."

"I know," Kate said. "That's why I want to go there."

Once more, the lightning flashed, closer this time. Anders stood still, looking around. Then he grabbed Tina's hand. Once more he started running, yelling at Kate to follow.

"Anders!" Kate wailed. "Where are you going?"

"Help me with Tina!" he said. "It's dangerous out here!"

"Then let's get to that tree!"

"No! It would act like a lightning rod!"

An instant later, a gust of wind struck Kate. Like a moving wall, a sheet of rain washed against them.

"Lie down!" Anders told Tina as they reached a hollow in the ground. The little girl dropped onto her stomach.

"You, too," Anders told Kate.

Kate stared at her white dress. "Lie down?"

In that moment, lightning flashed close at hand. Without

another word Kate dropped to her knees. As she stretched out, the wet grass soaked through her dress.

"Put your arms around your head," Anders told them, and Tina and Kate obeyed.

Kate squeezed her eyes shut. Water poured down on her back. Lightning flashed, again and again. Even through closed eyes, Kate saw the light.

After what seemed forever, Kate opened her eyes and raised her head to look toward the large oak. Again she wished she were safe and dry under the large tree.

In that instant, lightning hit the uppermost branch. With a flash of fire the lightning split the trunk from top to bottom. Like flying swords, strips of bark flew in all directions.

19

Nighttime Terror

*K*ate tucked her head beneath her arms as thunder crashed around them. Even the earth seemed to shake.

When it died away, Kate swallowed hard. "Anders?"

"I saw it." Even her hard-to-frighten brother sounded impressed.

Kate fought down her fear, but inside she was trembling. When the fury of the storm seemed to ease, Kate once more lifted her head.

"Anders . . ." Her voice sounded as small as she felt. "I don't like to say it, but . . ."

Her brother looked up. "You don't have to tell me. I'll remind you the rest of your life." The rain streamed through his blond hair, but he grinned. "I was right, huh? Just depend on me, your big brother. Smart. Strong. Always right."

"Smart aleck, you mean," Kate said.

"Taking care of you, my little sisters. In the future, just remember my good help. Instead of arguing—"

"That's for sure," Tina said. Her little face was smudged with dirt. "You betcha."

For all the world she sounded like Anders. In spite of all that had happened, Kate giggled.

"Yup," Anders went on. "You girls—"

Another torrent of rain cut off his words. Once again, Kate ducked her head. For a long time she lay there wondering when the storm would end. With each passing minute, she grew more wet and more miserable.

When the storm seemed to lessen, Anders said, "That shelter in Glen Park is closer than Granny's. Let's run for the park."

Down the steps into the ravine they raced, clinging to the railing to find their way in the growing darkness. As they crossed the bridge, lightning flashed, lighting the Glen as if it were day. Thunder crashed around them.

"Kate?" Tina asked, and Kate knew her little sister was afraid.

"We're all right," Kate answered quickly. "But let's hurry."

On the other side of the river, they scrambled up the steps. Soon they reached the log shelter. When Anders opened the door, it creaked on its hinges.

The moment they stepped inside, rain once more poured down on the earth. Darkness so thick that Kate could not see her hand filled the room. A strong wind blew water through the cracks between logs.

Kate led Tina to the back side of the shelter, away from the wind. In the darkness Kate heard Anders prowling around.

On the next lightning flash, Kate found what seemed to be a serving window for people having picnics. When she pushed against the wooden covering, it swung out like a door hinged at the top. Kake propped it up with a stick. The dim light from outside gave some sense of where she was.

The driving rain pounded against the roof. "This is going to last all night," Kate said.

"Probably." Her brother's voice came from the darkness. "But we'll be all right if we stay here."

"Mama's going to worry," Kate said.

"She knows I'll take care of you."

Kate hooted. "I suppose I'll have to live with the memory of your good help forever."

Anders laughed. "Yah, sure."

But his laughter was cut short by a heavy thud. "Owwww!"

"Serves you right, bumping into something," Kate said.

"It's the cookstove." When Anders found some matches, he struck one of them.

By its flame Kate saw a small picnic table with two benches. She led Tina there, then remembered her own white dress. Getting the dress so dirty was bad enough without tearing the cloth as well.

When the first match burned out, Anders struck another. Kate felt the nearest bench for slivers, then sat down. Beside her, Tina snuggled close.

Anders continued to search. He lit two more matches before finding a short candle someone had left.

"Now, gather around, girls," he said. "I've provided all the comforts of home."

"Aw, forget it!" Kate said.

Tipping the candle, her brother let the wax drip on the table. When he set the candle on the melted wax, it hardened around the bottom.

A current of air caught the flame, and it wavered this way and that. Yet Kate felt better, just seeing the light pierce the darkness.

As time grew long, Anders started prowling around the cabin again. Finally he said, "I'm going after Lars."

"You're leaving us?" Kate asked. In spite of her pride, the words spilled out.

"Something's wrong, or he would have come back a long time ago. I've got to find him."

Kate shivered. She didn't like the idea of being left alone. "What if that awful Leo finds us?"

"He won't." Anders sounded sure of it. "By now Leo's a long ways away. I'll tell Papa about Lars, and we'll come back with the police. You and Tina are safer here than out in the storm."

He was gone then, a silent shadow slipping into the night. As he closed the door behind him, it again creaked on its hinges.

For a long time Kate stared at the candle, wishing Anders would come back. Tina leaned against her, and Kate put her arm around the five-year-old. Gradually her breathing grew quiet, and she stopped trembling.

Through the open window and the cracks between logs, Kate could see the night sky. Whenever the lightning flashed, the world turned white, as light as day.

In between the flashes Kate felt grateful for the candle's glow. As the candle burned low, she looked around. Soon they would once more be plunged into darkness.

Before that moment, Kate wanted to know where everything was. Here and there, spiders had crawled in out of the rain. Kate wondered if Tina hated them as much as she did.

Then, in a space between two logs, Kate saw something black. What was it? A spider? But it looked so big.

Kate closed her eyes, then opened them, hoping it would be gone. But whatever was there was still waiting. Waiting for the candle to burn out?

For a time Kate watched it. *It doesn't move.*

The candle flickered. *Maybe it's something dead. Or even worse, it might crawl out.*

The candle was rapidly disappearing. *I'd rather know what it is now while I have some light.*

As Kate started to get up, Tina spoke. "What's the matter?"

"I just want to see something," Kate answered, trying to sound calm for Tina's sake. Yet Kate moved slowly, dreading what she might find.

At the wall she bent down for a better look. It wasn't a spider! Kate breathed a sigh of relief.

But what was it? Tucked between two logs, it reminded her of something—Linette's bag of diamonds!

Kate pulled the small bag from its hiding place. At the table once more, she untied the drawstring at the top. Carefully she lifted the end of the bag. A lovely gem rolled out on her hand.

"Kate!" Tina cried. "What a pretty piece of glass!"

"It's not glass!" Kate couldn't believe her eyes. "It's a diamond!"

"A diamond!" the little girl echoed. "Are you sure?"

Kate was sure. In the candlelight the precious stone sparkled blue-white. Kate didn't think she'd ever seen anything so beautiful.

Kate felt the bag and knew there were more diamonds. As she started to take them out, the candle sputtered. In another minute its light would be gone.

Kate slipped the diamond into the bag and tied the drawstring. But now she had another problem—where to hide the diamonds.

Then Kate remembered her only pocket, a deep one in the side seam of her dress. She pushed the little bag inside and stuffed her handkerchief on top.

The candle wick lay in a pool of wax. In the next moment the flame died out. Darkness closed in around Kate and Tina.

With it came fear. *There's only one person who could have hidden the diamonds here.* Had Leo pushed the small bag into the crack in case someone found and searched him?

In the storm no one could possibly have found him. *He'll be back*, Kate thought. *Sooner or later, he'll be back.* All Kate could hope for was that she and Tina were gone when Leo returned.

Sitting in darkness, Kate listened. When the rain lost its fury, she heard other sounds. Somewhere near her foot, a small animal scurried past. Kate jerked back, having all she could do to keep from crying out.

Then rain pounded against the roof again. As it let up a second time, Kate felt sure she heard a new noise. Was someone coming?

Soon she heard footsteps on the dirt trail not far away. *It must be Anders!*

Kate jumped up, ready to call out. But when she opened her mouth, something warned her. At the last moment she sensed something wrong.

The footsteps coming toward the shelter sounded different. Heavier. Too heavy for her brother.

Panic clutched Kate's stomach. *It's not Anders!*

In the darkness Kate found Tina's hand. "Shhh," she warned, close to the little girl's ear. "Don't make a sound."

When the lightning flashed, Kate peered through the cracks.

A tall body stood between the logs and the lightning. Feeling along the wall, the man circled the shelter, as though looking for the door.

"Help me carry the bench," Kate whispered to Tina.

Taking Tina's hand, Kate put it down on one end of the bench. When Kate picked up the other end, Tina got the idea. Feeling their way in the dark, the girls carried the bench to the window.

When they bumped against the wall, Kate caught her breath. She stopped to listen. Whoever the man was, he was close to the door on the opposite side of the shelter.

Kate reached out, pulled Tina onto the bench. "Climb out the window," Kate whispered.

Instantly Tina obeyed. As soon as she was gone, Kate climbed up on the bench. She had one leg over the windowsill when her dress caught on a splinter.

With a loud creak the door opened.

Filled with panic, Kate tried to free her dress. The large shape stepped into the doorway, looming darker than the sky behind it.

Kate swung her other leg over the sill. With the sound of ripping cloth, she dropped to the ground outside.

20

Race for Life

$\mathcal{A}$s Tina grabbed her hand, Kate started running. Near the shelter the trees had narrow trunks. With the next lightning flash, Kate spied a larger oak. In the crash of thunder that followed, she and Tina headed there and slipped behind the trunk.

Here, among a great number of trees about the same size, the possibility of a lightning strike was less. Just the same, Kate felt uneasy about the swaying branches. What if one of them cracked and broke?

When the lightning flashed again, Kate peered around the tree trunk. The man had come outside.

Leo!

As he glanced their way, Kate ducked back behind the tree. *Leo knows you want to stop what he's doing,* Roberto had warned.

Now Kate felt sure of something else. *Leo knows I was there. He knows I have the diamonds!*

For the first time in that hot July day, Kate felt cold. But it was the chill of fear.

Moments later, Kate felt the wind and understood why. She

and Tina had run away from the Glen instead of toward it. Leo and the log shelter were between them and the bridge they needed for escape.

"We'll circle around," Kate whispered to Tina.

Behind where they stood, the ground dropped sharply away. If they stayed below the crest of the hill, it would hide them.

Silently Kate moved backward. Tina stepped back too, her hand gripping Kate's. Just before they dropped out of sight, Kate looked toward the shelter. As the lightning flashed, she saw Leo coming their way.

My white dress! Even in the dark, it caught whatever small light there was.

Like the pouring rain, fear washed over Kate. Not only did she need to get away. She must also keep Tina safe.

Fighting against panic, Kate crouched down. As soon as the hill hid her and Tina from Leo, they started running. More than once, they fell and picked themselves up.

As the hill grew steeper, they clung to any branch that would help them. Slipping on wet grass and leaves, Kate and Tina slid downward. Partway down the hill, they tumbled against the trunk of a fallen tree. Feeling as if she could not move, Kate stayed on the ground.

Her head was still spinning when she heard Leo behind them. As Tina started to sit up, Kate pushed her back.

From somewhere close by, Kate heard rushing water. Leading Tina, she crept around to the other side of the trunk. Staying low, they reached the branches of the tree.

The next lightning flash showed Kate where to go. Rushing water had cut a zigzag channel in the steepest part of the hill. At a turn in the channel, sticks and stones and leaves had washed onto the bank. The top of the fallen tree rested on the pile of litter, creating a hollow.

Kate and Tina crawled into the opening. Lying on the ground, they gasped, trying to catch their breath.

This time Kate would not allow herself to look back. Instead, she and Tina tucked themselves as far into their hiding place as they could.

From somewhere nearby, Kate heard an exclamation. Had Leo bumped into a tree?

He'll keep looking. Kate tried to push aside her terror. Yet she felt sure of one thing. *He'll keep looking—even if it takes all night!*

As Kate and Tina waited, the minutes grew long. Gradually the rain eased, then stopped.

When the wind blew away the remaining spatters of rain, Kate wondered if they were safe. Maybe Leo had given up and gone. But where were Anders and Lars, Papa and the police?

Around them, the night grew colder. Tina shivered, and Kate huddled close, trying to warm her. Then she remembered the diamonds. What had happened to them as she tumbled down the hill?

Quickly Kate felt in her pocket. The small bag was still there!

A moment later, Kate heard the sounds she dreaded. She felt sure there was a man nearby. A man trying to walk quietly, his footsteps muffled by wet gras and leaves. Yet she heard a branch snap, then a curse in the darkness.

Just when you think everything's all right, Leo strikes again, Roberto had warned.

Closer and closer Leo came. Suddenly Tina sneezed.

Inwardly Kate groaned. *Now what do I do?*

She waited, telling herself that Leo had not heard.

"I know you're there!" he called out.

Kate laid a hand across Tina's arm. "Don't move," she whispered. "He's not sure where we are."

Tina gasped. Frantically she covered her nose and mouth with her hands, trying to hold back another sneeze. But when it came, it was loud enough for Leo to hear.

"Come on out!" he called roughly. His voice was closer now.

Kate put her mouth next to Tina's ear. "We've got to run for it again. Follow me."

Without making a sound, Kate crept out from their hiding place. Tree trunks were thick shadows—darker than the rest of the night. Kate spotted another opening between trees.

Down the hill they slid until Kate felt the dirt of a trail. She crept along, staying as low as possible. When Tina started to stand up, Kate whispered again. "Keep low."

With both of them running, they darted from tree to tree. From the bottom of the hill they could still circle around. If they reached the Glen, they would find the bridge.

Behind them Kate heard Leo crashing downward at a headlong pace. When she and Tina reached the lowlands near the river, the trees gave way to long grass.

Kate could barely make out the opening of a narrow path. As she ran, the marsh grass whipped at her dress and legs. Soon the path disappeared. Leo was getting closer.

Kate reached back, caught her sister's hand. Tina was breathing in great long gasps. Kate knew the little girl couldn't keep on much longer.

Then Kate saw something even darker than the grass. The river!

Instead of circling around, she had led Tina onto a peninsula. Soon they'd be trapped by the swiftly flowing water!

No longer able to push away her panic, Kate kept running. When the ground gave way to mud, she had to stop.

Frantically Kate tried to think. Desperately she prayed for help. But terror held her mind, like a captive unable to escape.

Then one thought came. Only one thought. The mother partridge. *If I could hide Tina—*

The idea seemed impossible. All Kate had was grass—long grass three or four feet high.

Well, why not?

Leo had seen her white dress, but maybe he hadn't spotted Tina. *Maybe he doesn't know that she's here.*

A few steps back, the ground was solid. Kate led Tina to the longest grass she could find in the dark.

"Get down," Kate told her.

As Tina tucked herself into a ball, Kate pulled the marsh grass over the little girl.

"Stay here." Even to her own ears, Kate's voice sounded hoarse with fear. "Don't move, no matter what."

"Kate?" the little girl asked, as if on the edge of tears. Kate knew that Tina didn't want to be left.

"I'm going for help," Kate whispered. "You'll be safe if you don't move."

Standing up, Kate looked down at her dress. In the starless night, the white cloth showed more than anything else. With her heart in her throat, Kate faced the widest part of the peninsula.

Leo was coming toward her. Somehow she had to get around him, draw him away from Tina.

Quickly Kate pulled off her shoes and left them behind. Darting to her right, she ran toward the edge of the grass. When she felt mud beneath her bare feet, she had to slow down. Yet she kept going, walking straight into it.

Leo angled off, changing direction to cut off Kate's escape. Once again he came straight toward her. Acting as if she had given up, Kate waited.

Leo was coming fast now, his footsteps heavy. Just before he reached her, Kate dodged around him, running lightly in the mud.

As she reached firmer ground, she heard the man's angry muttering. Kate glanced back. With his greater weight, he had sunk deep into the mud.

It's my chance! Kate thought and increased her speed. She had no doubt that she could get away.

Then she remembered Tina. The mother bird had gone just far enough to distract them. No farther.

Kate slowed down. Leo's footsteps sounded different, as if he might have lost a shoe in the mud. But as Kate circled the bottom of the steep hill, she heard him running again.

Kate leaped ahead, staying parallel to the main channel of the river. She had her directions straight now and ran as fast as her legs would take her.

When she reached the South Fork, Kate left the main channel and slipped into the Glen. There in the narrow valley, she had even less light. As Kate started uphill toward the bridge, she needed to feel her way.

Behind her, Leo was catching up. Kate's side ached now, and she gasped for air. *How long can I keep running?*

In the next moment Kate realized the path had washed out. Even in the dim light, she saw the dark water, the rising river. The rushing torrent tumbled beside her, cold and deep. One wrong step would bring disaster.

Circling a large rock, Kate dug her bare feet into the hill. More than once she stepped on something sharp. Feeling desperate, she worked her way up the steep bank. Her hands reached out, clung to trees, branches, anything that would keep her from sliding down.

When Kate reached the bridge, Leo was close behind. She was halfway across the wooden span when four dark shapes loomed up ahead of her. Whirling around, Kate turned and fled back toward the picnic area.

Footsteps pounded on the bridge behind her. Then Kate heard a cry. Her name!

Kate stopped so suddenly that she almost fell over. As Anders ran up to her, Kate drew long gasps, trying to catch her breath. When she couldn't speak, she pointed at the large shape coming onto the bridge. "It's Leo!"

At the sound of her voice, the man turned to run the other way. Anders, Papa, and the policeman dashed after him. Grabbing Leo's arms, they held him until he stopped struggling.

"Get over by that tree!" the policeman commanded.

Leo raised his hands against a large oak. The policeman patted the man's pockets.

When the law officer discovered nothing, Kate remembered. For a frantic moment she wondered if she had lost the small bag. Then she found it, deep inside her pocket.

"I have the diamonds," she said. To her great relief they were safe.

———

Because of the storm, the policeman had been helping other people. It had taken a while for Papa to find him. As the two men took Leo to jail, Anders, Lars, and Kate went back for Tina.

When they reached the little girl, she clasped her arms hard around Kate. "I did what you told me," she said, "but I was *so* scared!"

"I'm proud of you!" Kate hugged Tina as though she would never let her go. "It was scary for me too. Come," she said as she picked up her shoes. "Let's go home."

By the time they reached Granny's house, the rain had started again. For the rest of the night it beat against the roof.

The next morning the South Fork and the main channel of the Kinnickinnic River were running over their banks. People said the streams were higher than they had been for years. Culverts had washed out, and bridge supports were damaged.

One of those places was the railroad bridge over the South Fork. The morning train crawled slowly across to reach the River Falls depot.

When Kate climbed aboard, she once again sat next to Anders. She still felt excited. Leo had been caught. Roberto and Linette would get their diamonds back. Best of all, they wouldn't have to live with the dread of what Leo might try next.

Yet now that Kate had time to think, she once again hurt inside. After all the months of hoping, the years of dreaming, she had put M.R. out of her life. Her dreams about him had been so big that she ached for what wasn't there.

Just then Anders starting digging into his pockets. "Good old M.R.," he said as he pulled out a folded slip of paper. "He asked me to give you this after he left. Sorry, Kate, I forgot."

As she opened the piece of paper, Kate's hand trembled.

So, she told herself, *even though I did what I thought was right, I still care about him.*

M.R. had never signed notes to her in Minneapolis. He didn't need to sign this one. Kate knew his handwriting.

> If I ever change my mind
> about whether God is important,
> can I see you again?

Kate's eyes filled with tears. Slowly she refolded the note. Carefully she pushed it deep inside her pocket so she could read it whenever she liked.

While the train took them north, Kate stared out the window. Through the hills and valleys, the rolling fields, and the pine forests, she thought about M.R.

Finally Kate realized something. *He was the same as when I left Minneapolis. I'm the one who changed.*

Her thoughts turned into a prayer. *I'm the one who grew to love you, Jesus. The one who came to believe in you. And you're more important than what M.R. thinks!*

Strangely, she remembered Daniel. *No hurt was found on him because he believed in his God!*

Kate straightened, flipped her long braid over her shoulder. For the first time since saying goodbye to M.R., she felt peaceful.

After many miles, Anders spoke to her. "Are you all right, Kate?"

Disappointed, but all right, Kate thought as she nodded. But she didn't fool Anders.

"I won't tease you if you aren't," he said gruffly.

Filled with surprise, Kate stared at him. Suddenly she giggled.

"What's so funny?" Anders growled.

"You are," Kate answered. "I never know what to expect next."

"Just expect a really splendid fellow," Anders said. As he winked, his smile flashed.

"Yah, sure, you betcha." Kate giggled again. *I'll recover*, she thought. *I know I will.*

Then Kate remembered Darren. She leaned forward, speaking across Anders to Mama. On the other side of the aisle, Mama was feeding Bernie.

"Darren was so nice," Kate said. "And it's been so much fun having Grandma and Grandpa here. Do you think I'll ever get to meet my Irish grandparents?"

Mama looked doubtful. "They've never said anything about coming to America. But your Daddy O'Connell might have a cousin living here."

"In this country? Where?"

"I'm not sure if I know. After Brendan died, his cousin and

I lost track of each other. A few weeks back, I wrote to him. But I might not have the right address."

"Where does he live?" Kate asked.

"Michigan—the Upper Peninsula, the last I heard."

Mama shifted Bernie in her arms. "You know, Kate, your daddy's cousin has a daughter. She must be about your age."

Kate couldn't believe it. "An Irish cousin my age? Do you think I could ever meet her?"

Mama's smile held a promise. "Maybe we'll hear from them soon."

As the train passed through St. Croix Falls, Kate's thoughts turned toward Erik. In a new way she guessed what it meant to count on someone—someone who believed the way she did. It wasn't boring at all. Strangely, it made Erik more exciting than M.R.!

When the train stopped at the village of Luck, Kate gathered up her belongings. Outside Frederic, she moved to a seat with a window on the side of the depot. *I wonder if Erik will meet us!*

As the train pulled into Frederic, Kate leaned close to the window. A tall boy stood on the platform, his back toward the train.

Is that Erik? Kate felt sure that it was.

Then the boy turned, and Kate saw his face. At almost the same moment, his gaze met hers. A grin spread to his eyes. With his arm high above his head, Erik waved.

The moment the train stopped, Kate hurried to the door. She was the first one down the steps.

Acknowledgments

Have you ever stopped to think about all the colors you see in just one day? Most of us take our amazing variety for granted.

Yet it was different for people like Kate and Anders. In that time when dark colors were more common, the brilliant reds and golds of the circus, the glittering spangles, the spilling out of brightness, offered an exciting change from daily living.

In the early 1900s everything about the railroad circuses was BIG, STUPENDOUS, and COLOSSAL. Advance men covered an entire town with advertisements about upcoming attractions. People had more time to look and read, and the huge posters showed astonishing detail.

When the circus came to town, fathers took a day off from work so the entire family could go. People poured in from surrounding farms. Railroads added extra cars for those who were able to travel by train.

The circus was one of the biggest events of the year. For many, it offered the only opportunity to view elephants, monkeys, lions, and all the other animals we now see in zoos. No wonder folks liked to hear, "May all your days be circus days!"

Wisconsin has been called the "Mother of Circuses." Over a hundred of them have been based in this state, with six of these circuses beginning in Baraboo. Ringling Brothers was the largest

157

and wintered in Baraboo from 1884–1918. Cousins of the Rin-
glings, the Gollmar Brothers, owned another famous circus during the time of Kate and Anders.

While researching for this book, I traveled to Baraboo and the
Circus World Museum, which is owned and operated by the
Wisconsin State Historical Society. There I saw the world's largest
collection of circus wagons, the train-unloading show, and an
old-time parade. I listened to Joan Pierce play the calliope,
laughed with the clowns, and held my breath at the daring acts
in the Big Top. Along with children of all ages, I celebrated the
circus.

Fred Dahlinger, Jr., director of Circus World's Robert L. Par-
kinson Library and Research Center, answered countless questions. He also read a portion of the manuscript and arranged for
the loan of helpful books.

Sandy Edwards, a Gollmar descendant, helped me see inside
a circus family. Her father, Robert H. Gollmar, wrote the book
My Father Owned a Circus.

I am also indebted to Charles Philip Fox, the author of several
circus books, including *Circus Baggage Stock*, *The Circus in
America*, *Circus Parades*, and *American Circus Posters*. Thanks,
too, to LaVahn Hoh and William Rough, for *Step Right Up!* and
Bruce Fife and other authors for their *Creative Clowning*.

If you ever visit River Falls, looking for the places where Kate
and Anders walked, you'll find that time has brought some
changes. The depot has disappeared. Cedar Street has been cut
down to make the hill less steep. A swinging bridge, high above
the Glen, replaces the one washed out by long-ago floods. Buildings now stand where the circus pitched its tents.

Yet the warm spirit of River Falls lives on in people like Letha
Foster. My thanks to her for information about days gone by, her
recall of detail, and her enthusiasm about the town.

I'm grateful to Ursula Peterson for her walking tour of River
Falls, her work as editor of the *Pierce County's Heritage* volumes,
and her giving of her time. Joyce Breen helped me, too, as well
as long-time residents of the area, Bill Trebus and Sivert Carlson.

My thanks also to the *River Falls Journal* and to Joan Kremer

Bennett for her collection of historical articles, *River Falls: A Frontier Community Grows Up.*

By now the Normal School has grown into the University of Wisconsin—River Falls, and our son Kevin and his wife, Lyn, are among its graduates. In one of the University buildings, the Davee Library, you'll find the Area Research Center. Its acting director, Stephanie Zeman, gave me valuable help in searching out a great number of details.

Writing a novel often becomes a learning process. When one of my editors, Ron Klug, read about how Anders carefully picked up the baby partridge, he asked, "Is that all right? I was taught that you shouldn't touch a baby bird because the mother might then avoid it."

I called a man who has helped me on a number of occasions. Jim Hoefler is the Interpretative Wildlife Manager at Crex Meadows, the Wisconsin Department of Natural Resources Wildlife Area near Grantsburg, Wisconsin. When I described what Anders had done, Jim said, "That's what we often do when we band a chick. The mother won't abandon her baby. Birds aren't able to smell. The chick will just keep peeping until the mother finds it again."

Other people in the Grantsburg area also helped me: All of the librarians at the Grantsburg Public Library; Maurice Erickson, with his experience in the ways of horses; Sandy Fulton, with her knowledge of music; and Gene Gronlund, who is responsible for turning Anders into a stiltwalker.

I am also grateful to Ethel Oleson, the *Inter-County Leader* for its early newspapers, and Jill Alden of Frederic. Walter and Ella Johnson have shared their ongoing love and support in this entire series. Stuart Briscoe offered a key thought at exactly the moment I needed it.

Each time I finish a book, I wonder how I can adequately thank my husband, Roy, and my editors—Doris Holmlund, Ron Klug, and Lance Wubbels. They have given me ideas and helped me shape them. They have cared about me as a person.

Finally, thanks to you, my readers, for your response to the

Northwoods novels. It's fun to know that the Nordstroms have become real in your lives, that you laugh as I have laughed about what Kate and Anders do. I deeply appreciate your encouragement.